ASSORTED
FIRE EVENTS

DAVID MEANS

FOURTH ESTATE · *London*

This paperback edition first published in 2003
First published in USA by Context Books

First published in Great Britain in 2002 by
Fourth Estate
A Division of HarperCollins*Publishers*
77–85 Fulham Palace Road,
London W6 8JB
www.4thestate.com

The stories in this collection were originally published in the following:
"Coitus" in *Fence*; "Railroad Incident, August 1995" in *Harper's*; "What
They Did" in *Open City* and *The Pushcart Prize 2000*; "Tahorah" in *The
KGB Bar Reader*; "The Gesture Hunter" in *Harper's*; "The Woodcutter" in
Quarterly West and *Harper's*; "The Reaction" in *Epoch*; "The Grip" in *The
Antioch Review*; "The Interruption" in *Alaska Quarterly Review*; "The
Widow Predicament" in *The Ex-Files New Stories about Old Flames*;
"Sleeping Bear Lament" in *Bomb*.

Thanks to: The Macdowell Colony and The Corporation of Yaddo; The
New York Foundation for the Arts; Kathryn Chetkovich; Beau Friedlander;
DeAnna Heindel; Georges Borchardt; Jonathan Franzen

A catalogue record for this book is available
from the British Library.

ISBN 978-0-00-713756-5

CONTENTS

For Genève

ASSORTED
FIRE EVENTS

RAILROAD
INCIDENT, AUGUST 1995

THE DECLIVITY where he sat to rest was part of a railroad bed blasted out of the hard shale and lime deposits cut by the Hudson River, which was just down the hill, out of sight, hidden by forestation, backyards, homes. The wind eased through the weeds, pressing on both sides of the track, died, and then came up again hinting of seaweed—the sea miles away opening up into the great harbor of New York, the sea urged by the moon's gravity up the Hudson, that deep yielding estuary, and arriving as a hint of salt in the air, against his face, vised between his knees; he was tasting his own salt on his lips, for he'd been walking miles and it was a hot evening. He was a dainty man in a white dress shirt tucked into pressed jeans; he was the kind of man who had his jeans dry-cleaned; he was used to unwrapping his garments, chemically processed, creased, charted out, and sanitized, from long glimmering bags. Up the road five miles his dark blue BMW idled still— enough fumes to keep it going—parked far to the side of the shoulder so that it gave the appearance of being one of the many such cars, people up from the city for the summer night pausing to retrieve some lost memory or to taste the wooded air one more time before going home to the embrace of concrete. He was the kind of man who would leave his car running for the sake of appearances, to help lull an imaginary stranger into an illusionary sense of stability: all was right with the world, she would think, passing, going about her business; when he stumbled out of the car it was with her in mind—some strange woman passing on her way home—that he left it running.

Despite the aching in his feet from his awkward walk along three miles of railbed, he couldn't help but notice, hunched over as he was, the splendor of this place in the world beneath a wide-open sky, darkness broken only by the passing of a car on the road above him; during his journey night had come down upon him slowly, hardening over the course of several hours; his eyes had adjusted to the darkness and guided him safely to this place. He extended his legs and began to take his shoes off, edging the heel with the back of the other shoe. (He was the kind of man who untied his shoes first, removed one and then the other, seated on the little stepstool or else the edge of his bed; he was also the kind of man who used an ivory shoehorn to get them on in the morning, relishing the feel of his sock sliding firmly against cool smoothness, the use of an instrument for the simple task.) But this wasn't the time or the place for practiced rituals; he had come to betray himself, to rid himself of such things. He left them in the bushes, a lonely pair of fine, handmade Italians, one nestled against the other lovingly, front to front. He walked slowly.

Around the curve there was enough light—diffused across the hazy sky—to make out the shards of broken bottles (if he'd been looking down instead of forward). The piece he stepped on, from an old malt liquor bottle, was as jagged as the French Alps, the round base of the bottle forming a perfect support for the protrusion, the only piece of glass for yards, seated neatly against the rail plate; it went into his heel cleanly, cutting firmly into the hard pad, opening a wound that sent him falling sideways. It was one of those cuts that open up slowly into the possibilities of their pain, widening from a small point into a cone; this was the kind of cut that gave the fearful sense of being unlimited in the pain it would eventually produce; he sat there and thought about it for a moment, not making a game plan but trying to conjure up some image from a Red Cross handbook he'd once memorized. (It was a requirement for his sailing classes.) He'd learned to make a flotation device out of a wet pair of blue jeans; he'd learned how to stanch the flow of blood from an amputated limb by using a leather belt as a tourniquet; he knew to pull the tongue away and to clear the throat of obstructions before beginning mouth-to-mouth; but here, alone in the absolute solitude of his pain, he wasn't sure what to do except to keep trying to recall a line drawing of some kind, one of those sketchy but useful diagrams of some acute human misery such as a compound fracture, the bone just a set of lines protruding out of some imaginary thigh, two swerves like a Picasso sketch; he sat there and let it bleed for a moment, hoping the tetanus might drain out. It seemed his life had become a series of such episodes, long searching silences as he tried to recall some image lost to him, a faint diagram of a circumstance and the proper manner in which to solve, to patch, to bandage the wounds until further, more professional, help could be obtained.

In the weeded suburban outback, hunched on the endless steel rail (forged in Bethlehem, Pennsylvania, and laid down during the late nineteenth century, and used to move limestone from the quarries along the Hudson, to build the great foundations for the great skyscrapers), he removed his shirt and fingered for the weak spot along the seam where it might give. To get it to tear he had to use his teeth.

He wished for a single clear-cut reason for walking alone half naked, the pain from his right heel burning up his leg, the makeshift bandage flapping. An explanation: perhaps the recent catastrophic loss of his wife, Margaret, her car simmering steam and smoke upside down in the wrong lane of the Saw Mill River Parkway, twisted wreckage betrayed by the battered guardrail, the outmoded roadway paved along a trail marked out originally by Indians, the taste of her red hair in his mouth when they last hugged. A soured stock-option deal—his fault. The blame placed on a computer glitch. McKinnen's firm face behind wire rims, fingers prodding his glass desktop, offering a good package. His wife's departure one morning; her words of explanation shaky in black ballpoint; the name of his betrayer an old friend, Samson, whose handshake still lingered in the palm of his golf glove upstairs. Better stories could be told if Margaret had died slowly, a long decline as her white cells submitted, the shiver of her lips as they formed her last words. It wasn't reason enough for his actions. He was certain of that. Their large house stood along the river, excitingly large when they moved in, now just too much house; perhaps all afternoon he'd walked the veranda and looked out at the flat water until, around three, a crew of yard workers arrived, shattering the poetic silence with their blowers and shrieking weed whackers, driving him up to the third-floor office where, face buried in his palms, he asked for his own salvation—salvation not from grief but from something he couldn't pin down, perhaps just things he hadn't done. Perhaps steps he hadn't taken. Maybe he fully accepted that she was nothing but void now; she was skirts hanging in the closet, the smell of her perfume on the unwashed linen piling in the laundry room, recipes torn from magazines piled on her desk in the den.

Again a faint breeze came. He moved forward along the tracks, leaving a pad print of blood behind him on each tie. Ahead of him the tracks curved farther into the darkness; to his left and overhead, the steel girders and chutes of the stoneworks.

To the guys who spotted him a quarter mile later he came out of the hazy air like a wounded animal, nothing but a shadow down the tracks moving with a strange hobble that didn't seem human. There were four of them, their own shirts off, nursing a small fire of twigs barely producing flames but lots of whitish smoke slinging in the heavy air. Even in the firelight you could see that they were all four skinny in that deprived way, knotty with muscles and the blue-gray shadows of various tattoos. The one who spotted him had just taken a long draw from a quart bottle of beer and was gasping for breath.

Jesus shit, he spoke softly, wiping back a long black clump of hair from his face.

The fuck's this? another said, parting his legs a bit as if to hold steady against an oncoming force. His jackboots crunched on the ballast. He pressed his hands flat against each side of his waist. One of the others stationed himself to the side, running his own palms over the smooth-shorn surface of his scalp in a repeated motion half fidget and half habit; each of them tingled and jittered. They could tell right away that whoever was coming, shrouded as he was in the dark, was enfeebled and in some kind of trouble, indeed, for his shirt was off and he was swaybacking from side to side, maybe drunk or tired or both and ready to be taken, to be seduced by whatever they felt like dishing up; he was all their night had offered, like a prayer answered, something to break up the tedium of dope smoking and empty chattering and cursing and everything else, and they all knew it, seeing him, and were ready.

The spot where they hung out, just before the tracks carved a dark hole in the overflowing cliffside, was strewn with old railroad debris, rails and tie plates and gobs of black tar and broken bottles; it was an outback hovel se-cluded and safe from everything, as purely wasted and unneeded as they felt themselves to be and, because of that, were; a bunch of rubbish and torn-away flesh, the self-made tattoos brandished on their own young flesh. They were young, tight, and eager. What they saw emerge was a man softening into middle age. In his limp was a slight residue of dignity and formality, the way he lifted his feet as if they were still shod and weighted by the expensive shoes; or maybe all of that wasn't noticed until, coming up to them, he opened his mouth and spoke, saying hello softly, the vowels widening, the cup of his mouth over those words like an expensive shell . . . or maybe they didn't notice at all as they moved around him positioning themselves in silence, wordlessly, the guy with the smooth head coming up behind him while the guy with jackboots took one step forward and the others moved in unison to his sides as if he might make some kind of break for it. (That was the illusion of tension their stances produced, wanted to produce, were eager to produce.)

It was later, in the dreamlike reproductions of those moments, that he realized that the silence in which they worked bespoke everything about their young bodies: muscles limber from stunts, flesh marred and bruised and burned with hard little bull's-eyes from the butts of Dad-held cigarettes; the fuck you's of bodies being twisted into lockholds and half nelsons, pinned with knees in backs and sternums; bucked tendons and double-jointed bone breaks that sucked the air from their fourteen-year-old mouths in the recessed trailer park stuck down in the shithole wastelands near the town's toxic dump. These were the singing, mocking kids that he had feared before on walks in the city. Now he was happy to stumble upon souls rising up out of the darkness next to their pathetic fire. There was behind all this, as they worked in a silence

that also bespoke the kick that was to come first from the
man in the foreground, only the dull sound of the insects,
a sound so prolonged it was blanked from his mind and
filled in with a new, higher form of silence. The kick landed
in his stomach. He fell. Slowly and with grace the two
boys to the side came to him and gently helped him up,
feeling his lack of resistance immediately, making note of
it by bending back his arms behind him far enough to
produce a rainbow of pain over his shoulder blades. Their
job was to fill the beating with as much dignity as possible, to uphold the ballet of the scene, to make it worth
their fucking while—to produce a stasis upon which their
friend, with his long swatches of clotty black hair swaying
now before his bowed head, might work; and he bowed
slightly, directly in front of this shirtless man, letting the
little grace period well up between them—then bowing
closer and closer until his forehead was right up against
the stranger's forehead, touching it there damp with sweat
while he mouthed to him in the hushed whispers of a con-
fessor, a priest muttering penances, We're going to kick
your fucking ass, you know, so you might as well get used
to the idea . . . trailing his words off and offering up a kick
to the groin hard enough to double the man over, the two
releasing him on cue, so that he fell to the ground, his
bloodied foot swiping against the rail; the smooth-headed
one removed the wallet from the back pocket and opened
it, stooping into the firelight, fingering the thick bills he
pulled out, flipping the rest of the black leather into the
weeds, where it landed, lying open, spilling into the darkness identification cards, photographs, credit cards, and
bank cards that, when slid into the automatic teller ma-

chines and offered H H M H—his initials and those of his wife—would eject neat piles of bills, as much as anyone could want or need.

Blasted out of the hillside years ago (during the previously mentioned burst of enthusiastic rail laying) through a series of explosions that loosened the rock enough to allow men with pickaxes and shovels to labor over the piles, the tunnel was a ragged affair, a gaping hole dripping with springwater and a dank sulfur smell; it was a wound in the earth and the kind of place the guys liked to smoke their dope and even sleep summer nights, lying against one another and close to the wet side in case the occasional freight decided to pass through, swaying and creaking. These were ugly, beastly trains that spewed diesel exhaust and slunk along as if ashamed of the decrepit tracks, taking the flat grade along the Hudson River at a snail's pace; boxcars blemished and dented, the seals and emblems of their ownership scarred by weather, scraped clean, sprayed over— the whole hulking mess came through a few times a day, and even if the boys were in town, drinking or hanging out at the pizza parlor, they could hear it scream along the curve near the crossing grade.

It was to this tunnel that they dragged the man, yanking him along, his heels jumping over the ties, his mouth gagged with his bloodied bandage. One might wish it were otherwise, wish that these boys in their joy had decided to release him to the elements, toss him into the ragweed, the leaning stalks of wild bamboo, to rot or crawl his way back to safety; but no. The truth is that they knew as well as anyone what they were doing; there was here a scheme in place overall; the stars were aligned in certain ways and all was going as planned; if there is a God, and later, if the man was saved and taking on the deep question of his experience, he might chalk it up to (with the guidance of Reverend Simpson) a personal state of *deus absconditus*, abandoned in a sense like Christ on the cross; if there is no God, then this piece of blind bad luck began when he abandoned his BMW and started his trudge with great purpose, and no purpose, into the underside of the road, 9w, a road that usually took him on Friday nights to the city, over the bridge, down the West Side Highway and off at 72nd Street, to a parking garage of cool poured concrete, the thump of his car door, rubber against rubber, sounding particularly sweet echoing in those confines. At Lincoln Center he could park substrata and rise up into the concert halls without tasting fresh air: tonight it was Brahms's Symphony No. 3 with its mysterious second theme, the Andante that fails to reappear in its expected place in the recapitulation; and the third movement, of which he was particularly fond, Poco Allegretto, so rounded and soft at the beginning it would, if he had gone, remind him of the shoulders of his wife, of a moment twenty years ago making love in a small room on Nantucket, a fall night, the wintry nor'easter blowing with a nonstop consistency that seemed to smooth the outside world away so that there was only the soft wetness beneath him, and her shoulders. Of course, listening from his seat in the third tier to the right with his eyes closed he would, had he gone into the city, have idealized and sentimentalized that first night of lovemaking with the woman who was two years later to take his hand as his beloved wife. The truth of that night was different, of course: awkward kisses, teeth clicking; shame over certain deformities. He did not hear the Brahms and therefore he did not go through that particular memory. (And perhaps stepping from his car, locking and closing the door behind him, the firm crunch of his leather soles on the breakdown lane, he knew that he was avoiding this memory; perhaps, or perhaps not.) Whatever choice one makes in the matter, God or no God, the boys felt the force of chance was on their side; they had a duty to uphold, knowing as they did that this man they were yanking along still had some small trace of dignity buried in the muffled, flat cries he was making. In movies, eyes in this situation dart around, glint with fear, search the sky for something to lock on to—but his eyes wandered the darkness slowly and without resolve, as if cut loose; at the mouth of the tunnel, feeling the cool cavelike air, he became still.

He would re-enter the so-called world in a half hunch, with his knees bleeding and the sky overhead showing the first hints of morning; all insect life in the brittle weeds having fallen silent, there would only be behind him and down towards the hill a powdery hum of the conveyor belts drawing stone at the tail end of the night shift. In his pain certain natural opiates would have kicked in, chemicals that sustain the body in times of great trial and allow forced marches of one sort or another—great mass gatherings of the uprooted shuffling up dust that can be seen from jets passing, the ill-fated regions of Rwanda or wherever—those abuses of such extreme measure that we hold them out as testaments of a raw ability to survive physically against extreme odds: barely standing and barely crawling, he works his way thoughtlessly down towards a crossroad where, eventually, through good fortune and timing a kind old man in an Oldsmobile Cutlass will pull over, hitching up his sagging tan pants and tucking the tail of his white dress shirt (he's the Reverend Simpson of the Alabaster Salvation Church of Haverstraw, on his way to prepare himself for his morning duties), to greet this staggering vagabond. Perhaps because of some motion in the man's gait (again there is a certain control, even in this state of disrepair, perhaps because of the crease of his jeans or just the way his hair, although matted with dirt and dust from the tunnel, still had what clearly was an expensive cut, a layer that took care and time to acquire; whatever it was—perhaps just a goodly sense of duty of some sort, or a moral obligation rooted in his religious beliefs that *required* Simpson to stop for anyone wandering in tatters, decrepit, with the sunrise welling up over the river and his shoulders and the dew-slick rails and the road dipping down into a hollow of mist—he did stop, calling politely soft excuse-me's to the man, who on hearing him, and then seeing him, seemed seized with grief, falling to his knees with his dirty palms out and crying, breaking at that moment from his purely physical plight into something vastly emotional. It was the kind of scene that Simpson felt qualified to handle, holding this lost lamb by the naked shoulders, helping him to regain his feet and work his way by his own power up to the shuddering, ill-tuned Olds. In this beast of a car, rending their way along the edge of the river, one would hope for a conversation in which stories were slowly, through numb lips, related—not so much for the good reverend, who had little to say and needed only to nod kindly, to put his large fat palm on the leg of this shaking man, whose knees were covered with a polyester tartan blanket normally used for roadside picnics with his wife (for the good reverend was one of the last firm believers in the glories of the roadside picnic, being old enough to remember the days of the early autos, when the reality of the quick conveyance of the Model A was still somehow confused with the day-long adventures of the horse and buggy)—fueled by a lifting of weight and the elation and mercy of the pain he had traveled through: the death of his wife, financial problems, whatever ill might be construed as the cause for his act, a reason for walking alone down railroad tracks.

Last thoughts don't come easily, last thoughts rising above the shock and pain and the roar of blood to the eardrums and colors splashing behind eyelids, the ping of water dripping off the tunnel wall, the shuffled footfalls of the boys taking their leave, leaving him behind against the wall. The tallest of the four kids leads, yards ahead of the rest. Before going, he'd leaned down with his lips right up to the old fuck's mouth to test for any air and felt nothing, and to rest assured did a drop-kick with the toe of his Doc Martens—steel-reinforced soles of some kind of rubber that was OIL FAT ACID PETROL ALKALI RESISTANT and stood up to the toughest abrasions and work conditions, made in England, birthplace of the Industrial Revolution. His kick made the hard, solid sound of castanets snapping between the fingers of a flamenco dancer as the bones of the man's chin—a dignified sharp chin at that—did a wishbone break. He was leading the bunch, a few yards ahead, because he finished the fuck off and was entitled to his space. All the way up the river mists were rising out of the tidal waters, and here he was re-entering the world, shivering and clasping the sides of his sweatshirt before lighting up a cigarette, waiting to let the others catch up. The other guys came out of the tunnel light on their feet, kind of jumbled against one another, bumping and backslapping. As a finishing touch they'd gone back and laid the body over the tracks—an afterthought, a coda, a grand finish that would stand out as one of their great moves so far because it was certain to come, that one rattling beast of a train that always chewed up the last bits of silence the night had to offer, waking birds up and down the line, birds that would hawk and chirp stupidly in their sudden intense hunger; that train, an old New York Central engine repainted with Conrail colors, would haul a chain of some fifty or so beleaguered cars; they'd be down in the shithole diner tasting the weak coffee and eating eggs when the train rounded that bend in the river; they'd have their elbows fixed to the formica tabletop and the slick-headed one would be saying Fucking A, it's a fucking trip, man. I mean fuckin' A, do you hear what I'm hearing man? while the others nod and allow themselves a few minutes of silence—not even a nervous Fuck muttered—a brooding contemplation deep and spiritual, full of weight, or weightless of morals, of God or no God, as their stars aligned or unaligned, depending on how you see it. The body was found a half mile down the track by the engineer, who saw it first in the disk of his headlight and began the immediate emergency procedure for stopping a thousand tons of stock, air breaks and friction breaks both applied, turning away so he wouldn't have to see the impact—actually he'd never see it anyway, hidden by the front of his locomotive, but turning anyway out of respect for the about-to-die. The body lodged up under the coupling, or parts of it at least: divided cleanly, the legs stayed back in the tunnel.

By the time the train got there he was gone, either a skull vacant of chemical and electrical activity, simple as that, or a soul rising up through limestone and shale into the twilight sky: he was dead. When he died, shortly after that final kick, going deep into the shock that precedes systems shutting down, the train was still in New Jersey, heaving and bucking along the backside of Newark Airport, close enough to the runways to give the engineer a fine view of a TWA flight to LA roaring into the night sky, that morose exchange of warning lights going from one wing to another marking the wingspan. A kinship the engineer felt with all machines was provoked in him as he watched it, leaning down, craning his neck to see out the narrow cab windows. A tail of heat, bending stars, poured from the engines, curving off into the violet light of the refineries and suburbs as the tracks curved away and the train cut its path through the wetlands; it was later, perhaps in some recollection of that night, the body, another drunken stumblebum finished off by his train—it was his third such incident in two years—later that he would also remember the sight of that plane taking off; not that he *made* a connection between the two events that night, but he *felt* somehow that there was one between the plane and the death of the man whose body had wedged beneath what was once a cowcatcher and now was just a square-cut chink of metal frame meant to blunt the impact if the train did come into contact with anything. Because the truth is this engineer was a good soul who still wedded a romantic love of trains and what they used to mean—stretching their vast rails across this great continent—with a particular sense of the demands of the job. He had an ability to take the ever-increasing frequency of bodies lying across the tracks and turn it into a philosophical precept of sorts: the world was failing, spinning into something bad and evil, away from what once was firm and hard and, of course, united with steel and wood and broken stone—clean, white right-of-ways, timetables seldom broken. The full weight and burden of the death lay on the engineer's shoulders because he did not know that the man had been dead for a good twenty-five minutes before his engine sliced the body in half; of course he had gone through the procedure of stopping the train, applying the brakes, radioing to Central with the information, using his recently installed cellular phone to dial up the Haverstraw police, and so forth, but none of this alleviated the *weight of the death*, which he carried with him for the next several weeks not as a debilitating grief or a sense of guilt but just as a bad kind of feeling, a bothersome notion, that somehow through some miracle or grace he might have anticipated the body in the tunnel, known by some small sign—perhaps the plane lifting off—that a man would be in the tunnel, and therefore saved a life. In the late-afternoon light, as he drank his coffee at his kitchen table and prepared himself for the shift ahead, he thought of the man whose body had had to be pried out from under the cab by rookie police whose eyes—glassy and wide—had betrayed their shock at the sight, a torso barely resembling a human figure; by taking a spiritual triangulation from those faces, lit by emergency arc lamps and flashlight beams, from his perch on the beat-up Naugahyde cab seat (he refused to come down from there, refused to participate in the cleaning away of the body), he had known and felt the damage his beast of a machine had done, leaving a smear of blood and guts. And there, one morning at the kitchen table, in his house down along the river beneath the stone quarry, within walking distance of this latest disaster—with his wife in the other room singing to the baby and outside, down a bank of hackweed and brambles, the Hudson sheet-metal calm—there he sat trying hard not to hear all that music that was being made and had been made by his machine and the lives living around him, and the Brahms he had never heard before but was now somehow hearing softly, that Andante finally reappearing again but now as a solemn chorale. Evening was falling softly over the Hudson Valley. Fall was nearing. The air was cool and clear. His child was asleep. His wife came out in her jeans and T-shirt and kissed his forehead softly, holding her lips there, knowing what he was thinking about because he had been thinking about it for two weeks now. The weight of that death. But it was time for work, her kiss said. Softly, he returned the kiss. He put on his jacket, went to look one last time at the baby, to pass his thumb over her eyelids. He walked up the cinderblock steps to his truck feeling the weight lift. Evening was falling sweetly between the trees. There was the smell of the water, earth, sky. A barge rested in the river, waiting for stone. Down the street kids rode their bikes around in circles. It was a good job even if things weren't going the way they should in the world. It was a good, good job.

COITUS

THIS TAKES place on a Wednesday afternoon on the tenth of July on a cooler than usual day of a long dry hot summer along the Eastern Seaboard during coitus between Bob Sampson and Ellen Davison-Simms, who are lying together in light that seems to billow with the rise and fall of the curtains, which during those first moments (before entry) have risen and fallen several times, giving form to a front of Canadian air, cool and dry, bringing relief to two long weeks of record heat. The house in which our two lovers find themselves—as they say—is full of light, bursting with it, clean and white and not so large or small but grand in a way, attaching itself as it does to the larger estate it was once a part of; it's the so-called guest house, but it is larger than the houses farther up the hill, away from

the river, and now with the hedges grown up, the drooping roses on rotting trellises, it stands on its own. The
entry part is over—he's in her—and the rise and fall of the
breeze against his body—he's on top—makes his buttocks
feel chalky, like rock, firm and hard, eternal, holding some
coolness the earth requires, yet there is that line of his
suntan that gives him the feeling—at least a vague sensation—of being a man of two sides, one warm and the
other cold, hidden by Speedos and boxer shorts and tennis gear. But that's another story because by the second or
third thrust (is it a thrust or a wave, a movement confined
by certain latitudes?) the curtains lift again, billow, fold,
his head turns slightly to see them, eyes almost closed, as
white folds of light and space and air; curtains that his
wife made for the old house, their first together, laying the
long sheets of cotton in the living room to be cut down to
size—facing back towards Ellen, chin touching chin a moment, hummmm easing up from her throat, the nip of
her throat, he feels, vibrating—from off, off, the soft moaning of a boat horn, a tug, drawing a barge up the river to
the limestone quarries in Haverstraw, two warnings of some
sort, he hears them . . .

. . . brings to mind for no good reason Tom's death—his
brother in upper Michigan spilling a canoe along the Two
Hearted; a bad paddling river, lots of deadfall that spring,
water ice-cold, the cold black branches holding him under—it was at this great cost that Bob Sampson purchased
the depth of his eyes; Ellen saw that, it gave his eyes a
great attractive quality. They had met in that traditional
bump-together way you see in bad movies, or even some

good ones, where fate has actually transpired to physically nudge two souls together—or so you're supposed to think, at least, knowing damn well it's mostly luck and nothing else, what else would explain the quality of Bob's eyes having cost so much? You never get that in movies, the cost of great beauty; Ellen knew it when she saw it, met his eyes, in line; who wouldn't know it? Bob has great eyes. There is that deep pooling quality; they stay on you just long enough and then move away; he doesn't stare, but he takes some time with each glance, or at least he had, standing there, turning to order a double cappuccino with extra cinnamon—a man who likes cinnamon, she thought; she was wearing her lime-green skirt, pleated, tight against the sides of her thighs; she owned a clothing store and knew everybody in town but for one reason or another she hadn't met Bob, who was moving his business into his home, or setting up a home office, whatever they called it; she later recalled his wife; she knew her by first name, Cindy, a tall willowy woman who came in often and preferred long and black and somewhat draping dresses . . . we'll leave her out; the arch of himself into Ellen, that boat, the boat horn, her nub, the nub of her chin—pink and white light, cool, but nonetheless a thin moustache of sweat forming just above the line of his upper lip;

there is a reluctant sadness in the way he holds back from the next movement, what would you call it? It wasn't that he was thinking this but maybe the thought was forming anyhow—that it was a fending off of death, this pausing to keep yourself from coming, to hold off the spillage without letting on that that was what this pause was about, her hand webbing the back of his hair, which was layer-cut black, small specks of gray—maybe he didn't even know that, wouldn't allow the pretense of some kind of control into this moment; he wiped the sweat with his tongue.

what's the matter

nothing

you're sure

yeah

just resting

yeah

the horn again farther up the river more near Haverstraw, or just a train-coming-in-across-the-river sound playing those desperate tricks—what was it, a mile over there, two maybe?—the water glassy cool and slicked with silver; eyes open; Ellen, six years younger, still taut around the jaw but not clear-skinned, her own eyes hickory brown and small and close to his, maybe too close because he began the waves again to get her away, to move her back to get her to shut those eyes white and pink, that white-pink be-hind-the-eyelid thing; again the wind, going to the sides now, a nudge of his knee against her inner leg, the whole thing tipping . . . this groaning inward sound both made once, twice, the white lifting and the house, trying to re-move, to rid, to get rid of something. (There was this time last winter when, on the way back from the city, in heavy snow, going up the Saw Mill, he saw deer grazing along the roadside—no it wasn't what he saw that mattered, it was the monotony of the trip that did it; he was driving so slowly with the great windswept walls of snow blurring the headlights that he had to pull over to get his bearings, and then, for the first time in years, for no reason, in the boxed-in silence of the car he thought of Tom, his going down, the canoe tipping, the hard coldness of the water forcing his own breaths short.) What had he seen? His brother going down? No. Nothing of the sort. Just the red canoe wedged up against the tree, the hard black branches over the water and shadowed and down, too, you could see them; he dove down under after a moment to find—nothing—it was just hard darkness; the water current took him down, below it was much harder—then breaking the surface calling Tom Tom Tom, wondering if, maybe, his brother was playing a joke because he did play jokes. (He'd fallen through the ice once, ice fishing, goofing off, chopping the edges of the hole—but that's another story, just another story.) He couldn't remember a thing about Tom's face anyway, really, not any more than he could about Ellen's face really when he had his eyes closed and was swelling up into her. (The eyes, the lips, they come undone.) They'd stopped a few times to ford and move around the larger branches—too many times, really—and there were blackflies already that early in the day, already swarming; they'd brought face nets just for that, but they left them back at the camp; that was what he did remember, the smell of the fire, the cool hardness of the night, shaving in Lake Superior in the morning where the water was stupid-cold, dead-cold, it blued your ankles before you got in it. The way Tom threw himself headlong into it.

The logistics of the affair were simple, too simple, he sometimes thought, but not often; both were free, really, all day; to confirm her absence and her distance, to make sure she was really in the city, he talked to Cindy maybe midmorning, her voice tinny and removed on her speaker phone. (Between words, during the pauses, the machine replaced her voice with static; it was either her voice or static and nothing between, which made her all the more inhuman.) It wasn't that these calls didn't fill him with a guilt—the guilt was there, it manifested itself strangely enough in prayer. He attended the First Congregational Church, down the river towards the city, in New Jersey— a drive up 9w that hip-hugged the river—alone because Cindy found it boring and because he did not—as they say—feel like losing his soul, which he did pray for; he did, he prayed for the filth he was in, the deep blood-sucking void that he knew he had fallen into, if that's what you'll believe in this day and age—as they say—but it was true; he did pray for his own soul, and he did so carefully and with a dedication to making each confession true, frank, open to whatever forces were welling up and deciding the fates of souls at the butt end of the twentieth century—pink behind eyelids and the wetness and that hollowed-out space at the end of his cock, a cave opening up beneath him for a second then closing up; it had taken a while to get to the point of undressing before each other, months really, of talking and meeting for coffee; she wore her hair back, exposing the smoothness of her forehead and the thin pruned eyebrows; there was—he prayed—a meeting of souls involved that couldn't be avoided and that had led to their eventual disrobing, but that's another story, the actual meeting of souls—the wind lifts again and there is over his back the cool hand and the smell of fresh-mown grass, of bindweeds, of wild bamboo down near the boatyard, some faint hint of exhaust fumes, and she's saying softly into his ear, her lips right there, against the lobe, saying some faint phrase her own version of speaking in tongues, the cryptography of her own secret songs oh, oh, hooo,

certainly he did take advantage of her, he saw it right away—the potential for sex, for a liaison of some sort, for a meeting physically; part of it was the way she dressed on their second meeting, out of the lime-green skirt and now raggish; that day, late spring, jeans with holes in the knees and Ked's sneakers; when they ended up seated together and she bent her legs he caught sight of the dimple in her knees and from just seeing that smoothness extrapolated the rest of her body. It is certainly possible to do so, and he did it.

The noon whistle breaks open and you can hear it spreading over the shimmer of the Hudson, the tide drawing in from the sea, the deep-cut river licking the Atlantic, the Atlantic licking up beneath the bridge now, the sound haunting along the other side, cresting over the hills that you see when you're at the window of their room, French doors thrown open to a small tarred roof. The sound comes back and he feels the weight of the hill—still flexing, making work with his hands down there to feel himself and her around him, the slick, well-oiled mechanics of it— with that sound opening and widening; down in the depth of that river—it was a dark woody river—they'd slept at the campsite and gotten up with the sun, and after the shave driven twenty miles upstream to portage; in this he

found a place to put the blame years later, in the inane act
of putting the canoe on the roof of Mom and Dad's station wagon to drive back upstream just so they could
paddle down it (it was the only state-park campground in
that part of the U.P.—a shitty little dust-packed patch of
ground, creosoted hibachis ringed with faded Bud bottles,
a pit toilet to shit in), when they were already at the river's
mouth. The river ended at Lake Superior with a sharp
finality; it didn't fan out, or widen to a delta, but sliced
cleanly and neatly into the coldness of the lake. The plan
had been to canoe down and then fish late in the afternoon when the fly hatch was good.

What does
this have to do
with the pink lifting white of her hips, the flat of her stomach against his for a moment eyes opening up to each other
narrative thrust
drive towards
some resolution;
on the hill no one cared
for resolution, but down here near the river the music was
classical and folks cared
and even prayed for it,
alone
on the roadside
in heavy snowfall
praying.

Bob remembers hearing it, the shot that had killed a util-
ity worker who committed suicide up the hill in June;

they'd both heard it, lying naked—*the sound of a gun-
shot bouncing off the palisades, off the hills of the cemetery
up past the hospital; gravestone later marked, HE DIED VIO-
LENTLY BUT RESTS IN PEACE*—in a state of coitus in his marriage bed; maybe that was it, the reason he thought of it in
that technical term, because he was lying there in his marriage bed hearing some guy kill himself, just catching that
faint drift of sound while on that day the sun was bringing up those fresh scents of mint weed (it had rained the
night before) from down near the boatyard. Now, in July,
he's consciously working the pace, thinking how before,
shedding their underwear, drawing each other's down with
their fingers, her voice had sounded particularly lonely;
he was starting to see now that she was, truly, a lonely
person in need of him; a customer had come in to make
an exchange, returning a dark green-and-white print dress
she'd recommended personally, and, well, I don't know,
she said, I mean, Bob, it was like I took it personally or
something, her coming in, marching in like that, and saying it wasn't right—I mean it wasn't right, that's all she
said, and maybe I'm making too much out of this, I'm
sure I am, but, still, am I wrong to feel this way? she said.
Am I wrong, Bob? As if he'd know; as if any of us know;
and there is that working feeling now he should have
been lost in it, to it, just taking her for all she was worth,
but he's suddenly acutely aware of the wrinkles in the
sheets—which he'll smooth out, tuck tight, sniff and test,
maybe have the cleaning lady replace (this is Wednesday,
isn't it?); there was a moment in Barcelona with Cindy
when he'd felt this exact sensation—that the sheets had
been slept on before—and when he went down to speak

to the man at the desk he found it was true. They were in the wrong room. A used bed, perhaps made up out of some habitual neatness. His fingers are back around her, working there at the small flat of her back searching for something . . .

The taste of his salt moustache, the sound of another boat—the second in a chain of three barges coming up past Hook Mountain, rounding the turn up to the quarries—a boat horn might again bring him around to that moment, after they pulled his brother Tom from the water and he saw right off in the dim refusal of light in his eyes that he was gone, lost. But pink/white light, the sound of his heart beating, again another breeze, this one slightly tinged with tar—sweet tar from a roofing operation several blocks away, men with heavy buckets sealing up the top of a pizzeria—his rapid forward thrust, her raising up of the hips, the give and take, and that pink/white stare; the cool air; the hollow at the end, her soft cooing not even cooing but that little chortle sound you might hear from a bird resting, sleeping maybe, and they're going to give it all up for this moment, both of them, the dress shop and his business, opening up and the last ticking the smooth white, white stop, the pink opening, the lifting form of the air in the curtains and the tarred heat—as they say—the heat of the whole thing coming together; he'll be released; he'll lift the soul of his dead brother into his arms; the wet mat of his hair down over his forehead hours later when the state troopers, using long poles, took him out, caught him by a single arm was all it took, just hooked it under the armpit and yanked him out because you could see him right there bent and twisted and moving gently in the undercurrents.

Atonement has little to do with this story, that sound of the boat horn having edged its way into the waves of movement and touch that made up one afternoon's lovemaking. For a minute he had staggered along the bank helplessly, of course not knowing exactly where he was except that he was along the Two Hearted someplace (later, listening to Mozart, he knew the feeling: it was of two themes going simultaneously together, playing off each other with both a ruthlessness and a grace purified of all fault, the notes just taking, taking and giving, that was how it was there in the bland light, dark-branched, not knowing where, where he was); stumbling; crying; the wet mulch stench of the forest floor and the vast emptiness that the Upper Peninsula offers, that stony wilderness scratching the back of the greatest freshwater body in the world, a lake deep enough to swallow whole freighters, boats so long the crew ride bikes to get from one end to another. He was in that not-knowing of fucking and being lost in it, of the white waves of cold—about to come, going and lost—and he was just remembering the cost; she was, too, maybe, her eyes shut tight but his open—he'd opened them, he was wide awake, he was shutting them to the cool wet whiteness and pink of his own flesh; there was the tar smell, too, but that's not enough to make a story of, or about how he went a mile down the road, still-frozen mud, and flagged a pickup, a bilge color, driven by an old man with a hearing aid who had to be shouted into going to the store, where there was a phone; the wild assuaging of flesh against flesh of dishonor and guilt and a vestige of hope; for there was hope in coming for him, after holding back, and her pelvic thrust, too, and the dim prayer he had made that night along the Saw Mill; it's all short, the long and the short of it, and afterwards in the cool-sweat light, eyes wide open, she'd see the cost of it in his eyes, he assumed—the death of his brother that spring day, the state trooper's daunting eyes, testing, looking for some flaw in the story, the weight of the story already heavy, already breaking apart in his own mouth looking for the right words; and he sat alone on the bank while the men in hip waders pried Tom loose; that stony hand waving forever, burned permanently on the eyelids, the last moment as much as the first pink/white light and white and some darker purple as he clamps his eyes shut, coming, and she's saying I'm coming, softly, hardly air through the lips that memory has made, the mess that is, it has made of us twisted and torn trying to find these moments, the dark red flanks of a canoe on the bank, the pure wind from the north hissing through the conifers, the stupidity of going from one place to another just for the sake of doing it when you didn't have to—

it's later, afterwards, and still naked they speak softly to each other. She's asking for details, wants to know where it comes from, that faraway look, the long silences that aren't haunting but just there, a part of him, and he's trying to explain, on his elbow, trying to look out, remembering the time that guy killed himself up on the hill; he'd heard the shot, too, as did others, for it had come out of the ground and swung over the water, a report—the paper called it—bouncing off the inconspicuous ridges across the river and back—and it took work to pry that memory away, to start peeling back the edges, to find some way to let it go.

WHAT
THEY DID

WHAT THEY did was cover the stream with long slabs of reinforced concrete, the kind with steel rods through it. Maybe they started with a web of rods, then concrete poured over, making a sandwich of cement and steel. Perhaps you'd call it more of a creek than a stream, or in some places, depending on the vernacular, a brook, although over the course of generations it had dug a deep, narrow gorge through that land, a kind of small canyon with steep sides. They covered the cement slabs with a few feet of fill, odds and ends, cement chunks, scraps, bits of stump and crap from excavating the foundation to the house on the lot, which was about fifty yards in front of the stream. Then they covered the scraps and crap with a half foot of sandy dirt excavated near Lake Michigan, bad topsoil, the kind of stuff that wiped out the Okies in the Dust Bowl storms. Over that stuff they put a quarter foot of good topsoil, rich dank stuff that costs a bundle, and then over that they put the turf, rolled it out the way you'd roll out sheets of toilet paper; then they watered the hell out of it and let it grow together while the house, being finished, was sided and prepped for the first walkthroughs by potential owners. The Howards, being the first such people, bought it on the spot. His nesting instinct, he explained, shaking hands with Ingersol, the real estate guy. Marjorie Howard rested the flat of her hand on her extended belly and thought *Due in two weeks* but didn't say it. A few stray rocks, or boulders, were piled near the edge of the driveway and left there as a reminder of something, maybe the fact that once this had been a natural little glen with poplars and a few white birches and an easy slope down to the edge, the dropoff to the creek or brook or whatever it is now hidden under slabs of concrete—already sinking slightly but not noticeable to the building inspector who *has no idea* that the creek is there because it's one of those *out of sight out of mind things,* better left unsaid so as not to worry the future owners who might worry, if that's their nature, over a creek under reinforced concrete. So all one might see from the kitchen, a big one with the little cooking island in the middle with burners and a big window, is a slope down to the very end of the yard where a tall cedar fence is being installed, a gentle slope with a very slight sag in the center—but no hint, not in the least, of any kind of stream running through there. In the trial the landscaper guys—or whatever they are—called it a creek, connoting something small and supposedly lessening the stupidity of what they did. The DA called it a river, likened it to River Styx, or the Phlegethon, the boiling river of blood, not citing Dante or anything but just using the words to the befuddlement of the jury, four white men and three white women, three black women, two male Hispanics. Slabs were placed over the creek, or river, whatever, on both adjacent lots, too, same deal, bad soil, humus, rolled turf, sprinkled to high hell until it grew together but still had that slightly fake look that that kind of grass has years and years after the initial unrolling, not a hint of chokeweed or bramble or crabgrass to give it a natural texture. And the river turned to the left farther up, into the wasted fields and wooded area slated for development soon but held off by a recession (mainly in heavy industry), pegs with slim fluorescent orange tape fluttering in the wind, demarcating future "estates" and cul-de-sacs and gated communities once the poplars and white birches on that section were scalped down to the muddy tire-track ruts. What they did was cover another creek up elsewhere in the same manner, and in doing so they noticed that the slabs buckled slightly upward for some reason, the drying constriction of concrete on the steel rods; and therefore, to counterweight, they hung small galvanized garden buckets of cement down from the centers of each slab on short chains, a bucket per slab that allowed a slight downward pucker until the hardening—not drying, an engineer explained in the trial, but setting, a chemical change, molecules rearranging and so on and so forth—evened it out. So when the rescue guy went down twelve feet, sashaying the beam of his miner's lamp around, he saw a strange sight, hardly registered it but saw it, a series of dangling buckets fading out into the darkness above the stream until the creek turned slightly towards the north and disappeared in shadow. What they could've done instead, the engineer said, was to divert the stream to the north (of course costing big bucks and also involving impinging on a railroad right-of-way owned by Conrail, or Penn Central), a process that involves trenching out a path, diverting the water, and allowing the flow to naturally erode out a new bed. What they could have done, a different guy said, an environmental architect who turned bright pink when he called himself that, ashamed as he was of tooting his own horn with the self-righteousness of his title—or so it seemed to Mr. Howard, who of the two was the only one able to compose himself enough to bring his eyes forward. Mrs. Howard dabbled her nose with a shredded Kleenex, sniffed, caught tears, sobbed, did what she had to do. She didn't attend all of the trial, avoiding the part when the photos of the body were shown. She avoided the diagrams of the stream and lot, the charts and cutaways, cross-sections of the slabs. Nor could she stand the sight of the backyard, the gaping hole, the yellow police tape and orange cones, and now and then, bright as lightning, a television news light floating there, a final wrap-up for the Eleven o'clock, even CNN coming back days later for a last taste of it. What they could have done is just leave the stream where it was and buffer it up along the sides with a nice-looking cut-stone retaining wall, because according to one expert, the creek, a tributary into the Kalamazoo River, fed mainly by runoff from a local golf course and woods, was drying up slowly anyhow. In the next hundred years or so it would be mostly gone, the guy said, not wanting to contradict the fact that it might have been strong enough to erode the edges of the slab support and pull it away or something, no one was sure, to weaken it enough for the pucker to form. The pucker is what they called it. Not a hole. It's a fucking hole, Mr. Howard said. No one on the defense would admit that it was one of those buckets yanking down in that spot that broke a hole through. Their side of the case was built on erosion, natural forces, an act of God. No one would admit that it had little or nothing to do with natural forces of erosion. Except silently to himself Ralph Hightower, the sight foreman, who came up with the bucket idea in the first place, under great pressure from the guys in Lansing who were funding the project, and his boss, Rob, who was pushing for completion in time for the walkthroughs in spring. Now and then he thought about it, drank a couple of beers and smoked one of his Red Owls and mulled over his guilt the way someone might mull over a very bad ball game, one that lost someone some cash; he didn't like kids a bit, even innocent little girls, but he still felt a small hint of guilt over the rescue guy having to go down there and see her body floating fifteen yards downstream like that and have to wade the shallows in the cramped dark through that spooky water to get to her; he'd waded rivers before a couple of times snagging steelhead salmon and knew how slippery it was going over slime-covered rock. Other than Ralph Hightower and his beer, guilt and blame was distributed between ten-odd people until it was a tepid and watered-down thing, like a single droplet of milk in a large tumbler of water—barely visible, a light haze, if even that. All real guilt hung on Marjorie Howard, who saw her girl disappear, vanish, gulped whole by the smooth turf, which was bright green-blue under a clear, absolutely brilliant spring sky. All that rolled turf was just bursting with photosynthetic zest, although you could still tell it was rolled turf by the slightly different gradient hues where the edges met, melded—this after a couple of good years of growth and the sprinkler system going full blast on summer eves and Mr. Howard laying down carefully plotted swaths of weed & feed. (She'd just read days before her girl vanished in the yard that it was warmth that caused dormant seeds and such to germinate, not light but simply heat.) Glancing outside, her point of focus was past the Fisher-Price safety gate, which was supposed to mind the deck stairs. She saw Trudy go down them, her half-balanced wobble walk, just able to navigate their awkward width (built way past code which is almost worse than breaking code and making them too narrow or too tall, stupidly wide and short for no good reason except some blunder the deck guy made, an apprentice deck kid, really). She was just about halfway across the yard, just about halfway to the cedar fence, making a beeline after something—real or imagined, who will ever know?—in her mind's eye or real eye, the small birdbath they had out there, perhaps. What they did was frame the reinforcement rods—web or just long straight ones—in wooden rectangles back in the woods, or what had been woods and then was just a rut-filled muddy spot where, in a few months, another house would come. Frames set up, the trucks came in and poured the concrete in and the cement set and then a large rig was brought in to lift the slabs over to the creek, or stream, or whatever, which by this time was no longer the zippy swift-running knife of water but was so full of silt and mud and runoff from the digging it was more of an oozing swath of brown substance. Whatever fish were still there were so befuddled and dazed they'd hardly count as fish. Lifted them up and over, guiding with ropes, and slapped them down across the top of the stream—maybe twenty in all, more or less depending on how large they were. Then more were put down when they moved up to the next lot, approved or not approved by the inspector who never really came around much anyhow. Then the layers of crappy soil stuff and then the humus and then the rolls of turf while the other guys were roofing and putting up the siding, and the interior guys were cranking away slapping drywall up fast as they could with spackling crews coming behind them, then the painters working alongside the carpet crews with nail guns popping like wild, and behind them, or with them, alongside, whatever, the electricians doing finishing fixtures and the furnace and all that stuff in conjunction with the boss's orders, and the prefab window guys, too, those being slapped into preset frames, double-paned, easy-to-clean and all that, all in order to get ready for the walkthroughs the real estate guys, operating out of Detroit, had lined up. Already the demand was so high on account of the company which was setting up a new international headquarters nearby. This was a rather remote setting for such a venture, but on the account of low taxes (an industrial park) and fax machines and all the new technology it didn't matter where your headquarters were so long as it was near enough to one of those branch airports and had a helipad on the roof for CEOs' arrivals and departures. Housing was urgently necessary for the new people. The walkthrough date in the spring because the company up-and-running date was July 1st. What the ground did that day was to open up in a smooth neat little gape, perfectly round, just beneath the weight of the girl—which wasn't more than thirty pounds, maybe less, but enough to spark forces already at work, but that doesn't matter, the facts, the physics, are nothing magical, as one engineer testified, and if this tragedy hadn't happened—his words—certainly the river itself would have won out, eroded the edges, caused the whole slab to fall during some outdoor barbecue or something, a whole volleyball or badminton game swallowed up in a big gulp of earth. *There one second, gone the next* was how someone, best left unsaid who, but most likely CNN, described what Marjorie Howard saw—or sensed, because really the phrase seems like a metaphysical poem or maybe a philosophical precept (bad choices on the part of contractors, no not choice, nothing about choice there, or maybe fate or God if that has to do with it, one local news report actually used the phrase Act of God, if it's a phrase). But it was an accurate account because standing in the kitchen it was like that, seeing her go, watching her vanish, and all the disbelief that she had seeing it, the momentary loss of sanity and the rubbing of her eyes in utter, fantastical disbelief, would burgeon outward in big waves and never go away no matter what, so that between that one second her little girl *was there* and the one where she *was gone* was a wide opening wound that would never be filled, or maybe finished is the word. What they did was guide the slabs down, doing the whole job in one morning because the crane was slated to be used on a project all the way over in

Plainwell, and then thought while eating lunch from black
lunch tins afterwards, feet up on a stump, Ho Hos and
Twinkies at the end, looking at the slabs, the river gone,
vanished, the creek gone, vanished, nothing but slabs of
still-damp cement swirled with swaths of mud—the buckets hanging beneath them out of view—we did a good
morning's work, nothing more, nothing less.

SLEEPING
BEAR LAMENT

THIS PRAYER of lamentation—if you'll forgive the use of those words—began the day we were camping at Sleeping Bear and Rondo went out trashed and got lost. We freaked, waking up, about ten, hungover, blinking off the glare. Amy was in her panties in the orange glow of the tent, leaning over, working into her jeans.

Rondo's fuckin' gone, was all she said.

Whaaaa? Ricky said. It was the three of us in there, sleeping like so many logs.

The jerk never came back last night, she said, banging the side of her head a couple of times with the flat of her hand as if she were trying to dislodge something, fix a loose connection. Rondo was her boyfriend, and the panic edging into her voice made me a little jealous because I

felt an attraction to her myself, even though he was supposed to be my best friend; we played hockey together at
State and pounded each other on the back and drank and
stuff like that, putting on a pretense of buddyhood when
the truth was the real connection between us was shrouded
in mystery, or maybe it was simply physical: we were two
pumped-up guys, at the very prime of our physical being—we'd never, ever be as good-looking, as strong, as
virile as we were that fall. It was the opposite with Sam—
the subject of my lament—who was gawky and physically
inept, dirty and repulsive, his long, clotted hair flapping
like a beaver tail against his leather jacket.

That fearful morning I was sure we'd find Rondo's
drunk and bloated body washing up on shore, rolling with
a soft lollygag motion in the ten-foot surf of Lake Michigan. Those outside the Midwest think I'm fabricating the
height of Lake Michigan waves, just as the idea of a large
dune of fine sand in the middle of the country seems de-
lusional, as does perhaps the idea of love between men
who consider themselves straight, as I do.

I went out of the tent into the brilliance of an early fall
day, all razor grass and mounds of white sand and a few
tourists already lining the boardwalks that weave their way
through the sand; it was illegal to camp in the park, but
for some reason the ranger hadn't nailed us, or maybe hadn't
seen us, even though we'd slept—judging by the sun—
deep into the morning. If you did stake a tent in the camping area, you usually had to get up before sunrise to get
away with it. There we were, emerging out of the orange
fluorescent tent groggy and hungover, calling out Rondo's
name. Amy was far ahead of us, almost out of sight, in her

panic. In that blinding heat and light I didn't think of Sam's house down on Burdick, or Sam's body, which for all I knew had been dug up around there. I didn't think of Sam until we'd been searching for a good hour, going the length of the beach, walking past the carbonized relic of our driftwood fire, a wreath of red and white crushed Bud cans; going back up onto the huge dune, over that into the rippled swells and the nooks and crannies. On the edges, the trees somehow grew and then were tossed over by high winds to reveal huge, wonderful clumps of roots where you could hunker down and smoke a joint and feel this wonderful gradient of heat and cool at once, the dry taste of dust, the wetness of your lips. I didn't think of Sam until I was left alone at the end of one of the parking lots, seated on the top rail of a fence, face buried in my palms, giving up on it—knowing in my heart of hearts that Rondo was dead and gone and probably floating to Chicago, his body taking the curve past Gary, Indiana, the spewing stacks of U.S. Steel. There was a deep, empty hollow in my heart, thinking of his muscled torso and his witty grin and the way he could suck beer in those large undulating gulps of his throat. I like to think that in that moment I learned my first lesson about the idiocy of machismo; about how light I was, lightweight, lighthearted, and how the heavy-handed ideals of being a guy were ill suited to me.

Perhaps I knew that all along.

Because one night, years ago, after walking home alone from Sam's house, I went to my room and wept. That's how I like to imagine myself: an unformed little kid—a wide-eyed towhead facing for the first time the dark, empty hall of Sam's house down near the mills, that post-Christmas room of his with only one toy. I couldn't have been the worldly know-it-all who went into the house and smirked; who left only to tell the other kids that shit-pants Sam didn't have a toy to his name worth playing with, just a single Matt Mason space center, the same one everyone got last year; that his house was depleted, empty, and that when we went downstairs his old man, back from the mill—in his Elvis hairdo—was grunting down a can of beer, elbows resting on the table, face empty; that his first words were What's up, shit-for-brains? and that Sam, his face a bright crimson shameful blush, took me to the door and handed me my coat and went with me outside. Let's get out of here, he said. Bastard.

Did I weep?

Or did I go to school the next day and tell Ted Nelson, who was always looking for a reason to taunt Sam? Did I lay out for him a schematic of the house—the bald spots on the center of each step leading upstairs, the long crevice of broken wood packed with dust along the center of his hallway? Did I hand over to Nelson, like top secret info, the facts of Sam's situation: dirt poor? Drafty, broken windows patched with cardboard. A stalactite of lime stain hanging from the bathtub spout. Burned-out bulbs. Mattress on floor. A single fucking toy to his name right after Christmas.

On the fence overlooking the parking lot at Sleeping Bear I thought of Sam for the first time in four or five years, conjured up an image of that late afternoon at his house, my only visit, stepping into his kitchen to see his father, bleary-eyed, tired, wearing one of the olive smocks from the paper mill, a little round patch on the right-hand side of his chest with his name in wide, sloppy red stitching, ED; worn out and tired and bored and sad with life, lifting the beer can to his lips before saying what had to be said. The kitchen with its tall, old-fashioned cupboards that went all the way to the high ceiling; the countertops specked with the remains of a floral design; the walls and stove hood coated with grease splatter, embedded with dust; all of it illuminated by a bug-peppered globe. It came to me on the fence at Sleeping Bear—worrying myself into a fit over Rondo's body, his corpse out there in the lake—how we'd left the house, crossed the street, cut between the two buildings of the mill to the railroad tracks, and past them to the huge sludge pit where Allied Paper poured its waste and where all of us (in my crew) liked to play our witless games of chicken and dare-ya's; it was all very dangerous, the wide lake of paper waste that crusted over like ice and allowed you a foothold on some days, enough so you could venture out tentatively, then a bit farther if you knew it was strong enough to hold.

Gonna go? was about all Sam said, I think, standing there watching the way the failing light fell dead on the hardened corrugation of sludge. Behind him, in front of a line of haggard trees at the far side, winter birds dipped and dove over the edge of the pit. There was the familiar high-pitched horn of a switcher about half a mile away, coming our way with a string of stock; you could hear the shrill yanks of couplings. Industry was seething on all sides, but at the time we didn't know it, didn't care to know it, and for that moment we were just two kids silently daring each other to do something fantastically stupid.

The truth was that at the moment Sam wasn't really asking me to go but was talking to himself, to his bowed legs and his cheap nylon parka with the orange lining and the fringe of fake fur around the lip of the hood. It seemed more like he was saying some kind of prayer for divine protection, tottering there with the cold evening wind ruffling his hair while he toed the edge of the sludge—it was a betraying substance, not paper or ice or anything else, unworldly crap—and before I could say Sure, I'll go, and step myself, he was taking tiny little tiptoes out, testing the tension of the gook, feeling the give beneath his mud stompers or old PF Flyers or whatever he was wearing that day. He went ahead. He worked his way about five or six yards out. It was the farthest I'd ever seen one of my fellows go on the crusty surface. We swore it dropped off to fifty feet deep right away, dug at an angle. The switcher train was making its way behind us, flexing and tinging the tracks, and when he got as far as he was willing to go he turned slowly around and faced me and moved his lips, saying something, I'll never know exactly what; but his lips did move quite a bit, maybe five sentences, reciting for all I knew what might've been the Gettysburg Address, which we'd all had to memorize for class that year. Worn out and pathetic, in his cheap thin coat against a hardening wind, Sam, a kid with only a meager toy to his name, stood out on the sludge, speaking:

Four score and and seven years ago our fathers brought forth on this continent a new nation, conceived in liberty, and dedicated to the proposition that all men are created equal . . .

. .

Until the sludge gave way and he sank up to his knees—
the train behind me still lugging away but slowing enough
to make his cry audible now over the rattle—in a thick
ooze of dioxin and pulp, of solvents and irredeemable
chemical compounds. Like Christ walking on water and
failing, his frail, miserable legs cracked the edge of the
pulp as he waded back to me, the stuff gunking and cak-
ing on his jeans. One shoe (or boot) was missing when he
finally got out.

Trudging back over the tracks, across the road, he
scraped the crap from his leg with a stick and made me
vow never to disclose what he'd done to anyone.

You won't willya? he kept saying.

I won't. I swear to God. A stack of Bibles. My mother's
wedding gown. I won't tell anybody. It's between us.

I'd tell everyone I knew. It was a story too good to hold
to my vest. I'd transform the world with the image of Sam,
poor fucker, going down into the gunk up to his knees.
Except in my version of the story, I'd make it his waist, or
have him swimming through the stuff.

Amy called my own name, Means, and I turned to see
her waving frantically to me across the parking lot.

They found Rondo, she said, running a single finger
along the inside of her jeans to release some ill-adjusted
tension of her underwear waistband; I tried not to look. I
was awaiting the news of Rondo's life or death while, at
the same time, drawing into mind and memory the image
of Sam in band class right after I slammed my palm into
the bell of his cornet; he had the perplexed and bewil-
dered eyes of someone newly hurt, just before the pain

releases itself into a huge gush of agony; his eyes showed, I like to think now, that long wide leap to redemptive grace. Two of his front teeth were lost to the rim of the mouthpiece moving inward; all that force translated along the curve of the bell and through the tubing and concentrating onto the metal edge of the size 7c mouthpiece; I knew when I threw the open palm of my hand into the bell of his horn the physics of what was going to happen. I can't deny it now the way I did then. I didn't know at the time where my anger came from, but now I do. The lesson I draw from my own actions is clear: I was guilty of many sins before this kid, who, in band, in seventh grade, had already grown his hair long and was wearing stolen leather jackets. I like to think I broke his teeth over my shame; I had told the world about his house, about his father, and about his falling through the crust of sludge (after walking Christ-like on it for a good five seconds).

He's fine, she said. He was so drunk he didn't know where he was going and ended up in the campground sleeping next to the pit toilets.

She put her hand on my thigh as if to gauge my balance on the fence rail.

The great roiling swells of sand driven upward by more sand, compiled against itself; the eternal days and nights of Lake Michigan currents and the constant pounding winds rolling grain upon grain; the fronts staggering listlessly across the lake from Wisconsin like drunken louts, picking up moisture over the great body of water and pounding the coast until from nothing grew something. What did the Ottawa Indians think, wandering this moonscape, praying to their beloved Sleeping Bear as he lay prone on the great expanse of otherness, huddled against the lake? All along this side of the state the beaches were being taken away by the currents; houses tumbled down in slow-mo on the news, tag teams of bright yellow bull-dozers attempted to rearrange fate, and we smoked our cigarettes and drank a last beer and sat in a little alcove of razor grass and laughed at our fear, at the idea that we could worry that Rondo, all taut muscle and hockey arms, might be dead.

It was turning out to be a brisk, fall-like day. The front had swung through a giant line of anvilheads. Out of the firmament, the ceaseless drive of wind, Sam came to me once more: that day in his house alone in that room with the soft linty smell of furnace heat (What'cha wanna do? Don't know); the event with the trumpet. And of course his death—his death most of all—taking the whole high school by surprise. His cocky fuck-you's dead and gone. By that time he was completely one of those fringe beings, absorbed by the vast riptides of misery we pretended didn't exist; there but not there, a vanquished ghost of a boy barely making class but somehow hanging on, not expelled or in jail. The word around school was that he'd moved out long ago from the house on Burdick and was shacked up with some woman and her baby.

My lamentation began right then, taking a toke on the cig, blowing the smoke into the wind while Rondo and Amy tumbled back behind a clump of grass and Ricky did wind sprints up and down the beach to get the blood flowing back in his shrunken skull. I'd get up and walk alone down the shore and let them finish whatever they were doing. I'd get in the car and drive home with them laughing in the backseat; we'd turn the trip into the butt of a long, endless joke about our fear, and that joke would go on and on for the rest of our lives; but while all this was going on, I'd be considering those last frail moments of a life, and how maybe if I'd embraced him, coming out of the sludge pit, given him my shirt to wipe the paper pulp from his legs, perhaps things would've been different. I'd have changed the world; I'd have changed everything.

Yo, fuckhead, Rondo came down behind me and began drilling my back with the tip of his index finger. He wanted me to turn, to grab his shins and take him down. I was sitting right up near the water. The waves, good six-footers, were licking the tips of my All Stars.

Shut up, dickhead.

Yo.

You remember that kid, that kid Sam whatever, you know the guy who was, like, buried here in the sandslide?

No, Rondo sighed. It was a final no, a terminal no, the end-of-conversation no. He'd say that no and wave his fingers through the long flax of hair that hung down in his eyes; it was the dead-end no of Columbus's ship falling off the idea of a horizon.

The force of the mouthpiece against his teeth drilled his two front whatever-they're-called back a bit, damaging the dentine and the gum and nerves enough to kill them. The enamel turned gray over the course of the next few weeks and then, a month later, they both fell out. It was an accident, I told Mr. Tear, our band teacher. Blame was put on Sam's shoulders.

. .

You see, it was like this: he disappeared, like Rondo did that morning, except he really left this earth—lifted, unfolded his angelic wings, and flew across the great lake to Wisconsin. He was with some friends (that much I know), four other poor kids from our town, smoking dope, fucking off, doing what they do; he was with them and he went off on his own (or so they said) and then disappeared for a week. We didn't know this. If one of us had disappeared it would have made the papers, but for guys like Sam, to be gone from the earth for a short while was to go unnoticed. (He hitched to Chicago to see the Dead. His old man took off with him to the U.P. to go fishing.)

But eventually somehow they figured things out and sent search parties out to the dunes to poke and prod the sand. Men with long poles stabbed here and there, working in teams, marking quadrants with stakes and string. They were probing for the softness of flesh, for the give of a corpse. It took a week. There was a lot of ground to cover.

This is how I imagine it, and I like to think that it is more than just part of my lamentation. That it really happened this way.

It was a guy named Mel, a worker for the State DNR, a guy with long jowls, drooping eyes, and a perpetual smoke between his lips; a guy with sad eyes who lived in one of the trailers the state provided near the Sleeping Bear campgrounds; a man content at being alone with the sand and the constant sweep of wind through the slopes. He was doing a double-check of a quadrant. He had his own suspicions about the body's location. Years and years of being a ranger had given him a sixth sense about the way the sand shifted; he felt the areas that were waiting to give, the places where slides might occur. He went to his spot and looked skyward before putting the probe into the sand. There were four gulls marking the dark sky of late evening. He took a deep breath and said a wordless prayer and put the probe down into the sand a few feet and felt the soft give and knew right then that it had been his destiny to discover the dead boy's body; knew that he'd stand to the side while the rest of the men—the forensics folks and the experts—came in to finish the job, their spades making hissy sighs while he had a smoke and watched another clump of gulls come in to feed on the fish, dead from the hot wash of the power plant a hundred miles downstate. He'd finish the smoke, say so long to Mike, his boss, and walk slowly down the trail to the back of the park. (He could've driven but preferred to walk the thin wobbly trail alone.) On the way he'd think of his own son, living with his wife in Paw Paw, and how much he feared for him in the same way that he was sure some father, somewhere, had feared for the soul of his poor boy. He'd stop for a moment, hearing something in the brush, a tern, or a sparrow, or maybe some kids making out, and in that moment he'd say a kind of prayer for the dead soul and bow in his own way before the great forces of nature that had produced this huge swell of sand along the mitten of the state, and that had somehow conspired to find a way to kill a kid who was probably in no way expecting to die in a sandslide. What is fantastic about this moment, I think, is that in it Sam will have received more love than ever before in his life: that great profound love of the father for the son that we all need, a love greater than I, or his own nasty father, or anybody on the earth now living ever provided him.

I have to imagine all this and leave it at that while Rondo, back in the dunes, screams my name through the wind and calls me a fuck and asks me to get up off my ass and get going because we have to get the tent down and get packed up and home so he can be there for the kickoff of the Notre Dame game. He keeps yelling, his voice fuzzed by the wind and the surf, and I just sit there and think about how I'll have to come back here on my own, drive the four hours back after I drop them off, and find this same spot so I can commune with Sam, find a way to say I'm sorry. And I will, I think, I'll come back here and sit and go over the whole thing; the moment I stood in the doorway to his room—not the person I am now, and not some heartfelt kid, but someone still dulled by the vast desolation of that room with the Matt Mason space station in the middle of it, the little slab of mattress in the corner, the flexing membrane of cardboard in the window reading the breath of cold winter air pulsing on that part of the city on that particular day.

Back on this spot, I'll lament those two front teeth, which of course he was never able to have fixed or replaced. He died without them, swallowed whole by the earth one summer afternoon while his friends made moon-walk bounds down the side of the great dune, stretching their arms skyward, feeling relieved of gravity for a few seconds during each bound—stoned on bennies and acid and loneliness, the smoking cigarettes between their lips streaming tracer paths that zigzagged wildly against the blue sky.

THE
REACTION

LATE IN the afternoon Sloan thought he was having an allergic reaction, anaphylaxis, an instantaneous—in medical terms, although it might take twenty minutes to begin—violent reaction of the body's defenses against the allergen; all-out attack, was how he thought of it, an immediate overdrive of the bodily functions causing severe muscular constriction—including, of course, the muscles around the throat. He'd been reading in the journals about such reactions. In truth, what he was really experiencing at that moment was ulcers in his throat, a reaction to a pain medication he was taking, containing a few similar symptomatic indicators. A whole different matter. Common stuff. No big deal. Just lower the dose or change over to Advil. It took him only a few seconds to make the proper diagnosis.

Twilight bled over the trees in his backyard. In the orchard, past the stone wall, a dog was barking, the bark wrapped in silence because the road through the trees— normally a busy hiss at this hour—was closed to traffic. His neighbor, Congers, was having his house moved; the old monstrosity lumbered down the center of the street, scraping the upper reaches of trees, at four miles an hour, the paper reported the next day, but Sloan figured it must've been three miles an hour because it took more than two hours to get the house to the new lot, which was six miles away. (There was a photo in the paper that showed the house in the center of the road, with an accompanying article that made the move sound glorious and profound, an attempt to salvage the past, when in truth it was an act of greed.) Congers was selling seventy-five acres of prime orchard land that had been deeded to his ancestors by George III, along with six hundred fruit-yielding trees, stone terracing, a rickety farm stand, several outbuildings, a hand-operated cider press that had been in service for over a hundred years, and a view of the valley down to the river—all this was to be subdivided into clumps of high-income housing for senior citizens. The orchard embraced the south and east side of Sloan's five-acre parcel, financed by years of commuting the hundred-mile round trip to a hospital in the city. That practice had gone on for thirty years. Now he was running a small office just up the road, covering about two hundred patients, barely making it with the large insurance premiums, not making a profit at all, often living for months off early withdrawals on his retirement fund.

At the moment of panic, seated in a leather armchair,

facing a view of dying trees falling against each other at odd, disjointed angles, he was thinking about Congers, who the morning before had come in for an exam, a complete physical, the works (to make sure he was able to handle the stress of the house-moving project), and had stood before him—as a million others had before—with his aged body, his flabby pectorals hanging limp, and his gullet, thick and long; not to mention the wide-ranging liver spots on forearms and hands.

You're fit as a fiddle, he told Congers. Nothing at all to worry about. For a ninety-year-old you are in supreme shape, indeed. Except, perhaps—well, just perhaps, it's not exactly certain, but I do see some indications—from what you've told me—that there might be a gallstone problem. As you inform me you're having troubles digesting fish . . .

Sloan found it hard to divide the moment when he was first feeling the ulcer in his throat from his sudden awareness of the silence on the road.

It was a profound moment, indeed, he told Jenny, during dinner that evening, sitting at one of the restaurant's outside tables.

And why was that?

Well, it was because I was thinking of Congers, or at least I *think* I was thinking about him, and his house *was* being moved, and at the same time I was feeling this sensation in my throat, and, I have to admit, beginning to panic, wondering if the pistachio I'd eaten—one of those red ones—had caused a reaction.

And the house was being moved.

Right, right, yeah, the house was being moved. My

view was being destroyed. And our property was starting to lose its value.

So maybe that sparked the thought of Congers coming in for his physical.

You see, you see it's the fact that I told him about the gallstone. It's probably nothing. I mean nothing just because he can't digest fats. Who can? He was at the Cape and ate one of those, you know, those fried fish dinners—little plaid red and white cardboard dish—and he felt funny, those are his words; typical, nothing exactly specific in that, is there? Can't tell you the hundreds of times I hear someone come in with a big complaint, but when I ask them to tell me what exactly feels funny, they can't nail it. It's just, something feels funny. I feel funny. Just funny. We all feel funny, I want to tell them. We all feel really, really funny.

So you told him? So what? She touched her hair, just in the back, neatened it up. Freshly cut. Still brunette but patchy gray along the ends.

Yeah, but you see, normally I wouldn't have told him, just no point in it. Tests have to be done, and someone his age, normally I wouldn't bother unless there were more indications, aside from having trouble with fats, and so on . . . but I come right out and say, Sit up Frank, sit a moment, and let me check, do you want a drink of water? I give him a drink from the sink and tell him not to worry, but he looks, well, Jenny, I have to say I could tell he was worried because tough as he is, tough as nails, he's a worrier when it comes to his health (Probably why the old guy's hanging in so long. Living alone in that monstrosity.) So I tell him, Look, Frank, I'm concerned about this fish dinner—it's an indication perhaps that we have a gall-stone problem, and who knows what else. I give him a prod, I make him lie back on the table and, well, poke the hell out of him, both sides, thump him all the way up, back, not for any good reason, see, but to make him, well, I don't know, to make him think . . .

Jenny held her glass up and waved it. The point, the point, she said.

The point is I have to wonder if I was telling him, you know, just to get him, to throw him off.

He touched his tie, fat tight knot, stripes white and red.

To get him to maybe postpone moving that house, so we could get those lawyers from what is it? Save the Earth? Preserve the Land? You know, the folks who go around buying land and then just let it grow to meadow or sec-ond-growth forest, or swamp. Just to give them a couple of days. Because that restraining order, the one the land group, the one about the river basin and all that, might've come through. He'd still be there. And the house still be-ing there might sway the judge. You know. The house hadn't been moved, yet, and the whole thing is still in process, judge might just throw it out. Judge Janson, is it? Janson's old blood, tied to Congers, believe me; blood going back to old King George himself, right? He comes to me for a physical. The man knows the whole county. Says Janson, I know we're different, politically, but when it comes to my health I trust you like you're one of our own.

Along the curbside a motorcycle was parked; two get-ting off in leather jackets.

Is that Janet? she says, her voice catching. It couldn't be Janet. Could it be Janet?

For a moment they watch the girl remove her helmet, speckled azure with a heavy dark visor to cover her face, slowly lifting it off, shaking a waterfall of black locks around her shoulders. How did she tuck so much hair up there in the helmet? They both wonder. Then they think: that's not our beloved Janet, our daughter, who is lost to the elements, general wildness, not too wild, but always on the move and going from one place to the other. Our Janet.

Sloan took a deep long sip of his drink, and then another and then a quick little one and decided there would be no point in going further with the topic. Not that he wanted to shield his wife from the truth; just keep some balance between what was in his mind and what he spoke aloud. He didn't tell her the following: that there had been that afternoon a small sliver of time between when he felt his throat begin to constrict and when he made the proper diagnosis (of the ulcer resulting most likely from the pain medication he was on for his joints); that in that small fraction of time he had panicked (looking out through the trees, falling every which way) and a void had opened up, a wide space revealing what might eventually yawn into a crevice and, with oncoming years, become an immense chasm: a loss of his abilities at making a brisk, proper, correct diagnosis, a careful balance of professional opinion with the symptoms available. In that panic came, he felt, what can only be called (as he sat drinking his vodka) the first slippage in his talents. Beneath him, life was giving way. Night was descending. The waitress came up and cleared the plates and offered up several desserts: cream puffs, cocoa mousse, ice cream cake. It went unsaid. The fear that he was reaching the end of his long career; the deep welling sense of loss he had when he felt his throat at that moment. His utter confusion over the whole thing.

Between them the silence contained his throat problems, Congers's house moving, the parcel of land that was being sold, and Janet. Janet stood unspoken between them. The dew point was rising. The glasses of ice water were dappled with sweat. Sloan ran his finger along the side of his glass, tracing a small cursive *s*, and looked past his wife to the street. Behind them the Hudson palisades rose, weighty against the back of the restaurant. The river, down past the other side of the street, moved with the grand solemnity of incoming tidal currents.

Janet, he began, softly.

No, she said. Let's not go there. Not now. Please.

The mention of her name conjured up an image of his daughter standing on the corner of 4th and Bowery, the violet light-wash of sky overhead, pale and delicate with long shoulders and hair that seemed perpetually wind-tangled, deep, dark brown against the paleness of her face. With this, he recalled the fine little shells of her ears along her head and her hair, as a child, flaring with static as he ran the brush along the full length, taking care not to press the bristles down too hard—her bony little body taking the weight of his brush strokes, hips without a waist, straight on both sides, holding herself prim and firm.

He raised two fingers against each other to summon a second vodka, this one with a smidgen of tonic.

Another man came in for an appointment that afternoon with a pain in the gut, which Sloan immediately thought—

pushing his index finger deep into the right spot—was most likely a seed stuck in his diverticuli, a sesame seed, or a poppy seed that had gone its way down the intestine only to lodge in one of the little extended bypasses (he'd questioned the man long about his eating habits, not finding seeds, except perhaps a buttered roll he had eaten— he wasn't sure—for lunch a couple of days ago in a deli off 42nd, that might or might not have had poppies); the man's pain wasn't acute, but a dull throbbing with small peaks of acute, hard to quantify . . . and he'd said to wait a day or two and then, if the pain continued, they'd have to go in to explore—putting, as he spoke, one hand on the patient's shoulder. Sloan wasn't a touchy-feely doctor, but he felt it was important to impart at least one physical contact per visit, to translate his concern for the well-being and general health of each patient into something solid, a handshake that lingered a moment, a touch of the shoulder (as with this patient), even a rub of the knee in the right cases; for the really old, close patients, those who had been coming in regularly and to whom he had a rapport built on bad colds and broken bones and cancers treated and cured, rectums with fissures, scrotums with lumps, backs with humplike formations, jaw infections spreading in the brain cavity, stress fractures and torn ten-dons from gamesmanship—to these souls he often gave a departing hug, or a hug in greeting *and* a departing hug; and to his close friends, male and female, he thought, at the café, taking a second very quick sip of his vodka (hardly a bit of tonic in this one), he did give a kiss, on the lips or cheek, or both. As with his daughter the last time they met for dinner, he had given her a handshake, a pat on the shoulder, a hug, and a kiss on the cheek, and then the forehead; then, crying, he kissed the very center of her forehead where he used to put his lips freely when she was a small child (and so on and so forth), and then he kissed her lips, a real kiss, firm forward pressure lasting a few seconds, and imparted on her his words of advice, his warnings to take care, his hope that she would find some secure place in this world and, if need be, call on him for any kind of help she might need.

But really, I suppose we must not avoid it, she was saying, regarding Janet, the word, the name itself. There had been an immeasurable silence when the waitress delivered the drink. Silence between sips. The girl with the motorcycle helmet was back, putting her hair up with both hands, her elbows cocked in the air; her boyfriend, or friend, was beside her in a long black leather coat, helping; he had two rubber bands around his wrists, and he clutched the mane of hair, the girl's hands helping, too, and drew a rubber band down his hand and into her hair, twisting it around, doubling it, and then doing it again until that spot was tight; then he folded the ponytail in half and slid a second rubber band down (her hands all the while padding, adjusting the formation, entwining with his hands), until the whole arrangement was ready, and he lowered the helmet gently onto her head—both hands holding it from the sides—making small adjustments in the lowering process as he moved it down. She lifted her foot slightly in what seemed to be the beginning of an arabesque (many ballerinas lived up in the palisades, with large windows giving way to a view of the Hudson, the lights of Westchester, and from some vantages, the city itself). Helmeted, framed by the safety device, her face divine and pure in the candlelight thrown up from the tables, the girl turned and kissed the man, who in turn put his open hands around the thin bottom of her jaw and held her for a moment. He then straddled the bike, kicked up the kickstand, which gave way to the heavy sway of metal beneath him and made his arms stand out strongly on the handles. He gave it a firm jounce. The engine roaring (and it did roar, ear-popping mufflerless roar), she got on and hooked up her legs and, slickly, despite the noise, almost as if in silence, they cut out into the road and were gone, lost forever, the two of them, rest assured, never to be seen again by Sloan or his wife, who hadn't watched a bit of this scene, her back to it, and was still talking about Janet (what might or might not happen to her), stating emphatically that they must *not* put aside their pains; that pain must be dealt with head-on, her voice a bit drunk, that it was very important that he, Sloan, face the fact that their daughter might be a junkie (as if he hadn't), and also face Congers, go tell him to his face how you're feeling, gallstone be damned. The whole while he—not hearing much of what she was saying—kept his eyes down the street, on the place where the taillight of the motorcycle had slid away into the dark.

To get home they drove the back road that skirted Congers's property—a road zoned to remain two lane and quaint because along it lived those who respected the idea of two lanes itself, a road that had been accused only recently of killing four teenage kids. (Sloan was working that night, doing rounds, when the emergency room burst into life and the boy—the youngest of the group—was brought in with his arm missing and only half his face there, still alive, gasping, convulsing.) On the way home the bursitis in his knees made even the slight pressure on the accelerator almost unbearable. Maybe that's it, he thought. Maybe the evil thing about pain is that it makes us sensitive to the smallest nuances of movement; the urge of a toe-pressure on the rubber pad of the Volvo's accelerator, nothing at all, a thing you do your whole life without thinking, suddenly acutely real and complex; maybe that was it. Maybe Janet herself, with all her sensitivities, felt such things and couldn't bear them. He held this idea, taking the rolling turns, passing the crash sight (a chalk x on the tree trunk, which despite its having outlived the kids, the car impact, and countless rough winters, would have to be cut down; a small clump of wild buttercups and a cross (although two of the four dead had been Jewish)). He held the idea of someone living with an acute awareness of things like a foot working a car accelerator. He held the idea of fear, panic, and pain, too, combined as they were that afternoon when he felt the constriction in his throat. He held the idea that Janet might be an acute feeler, like those huge concave spaces carved out of the rain forest and strung with wires, collecting faint radio pulses from the very darkest, remotest reaches of the universe. He held the idea that perhaps it had been perfectly right to scare Congers about the gallbladder problem, to put the truth into his ears. And he held the idea that maybe it would be better from now on to no longer urge his patients into wellness along the smoothest lines, but rather to cut into them with the exact news of their ill-being. He held on to the idea of pain itself as the center of the world, the location of its gravitas. He held onto the idea that there was nothing he could do for Janet, his beloved daughter. Janet sliced head-long into the world heedless of what she was doing to it. They were passing the empty spot where Congers's house had stood that morning, now a prone monolith of dark-ness darker than the earth—a dark rectangle of nothing—and starlit gnarls of trees and the terraced land that would, in a few months, hold compact knots of houses, units, stacked against each other, painted that strange dull blue-gray. He held on to these ideas as he pulled into the drive-way, set the automatic door to rising, and then drove down beneath the house, into the garage smelling of freon from the freezer (they kept meat stocked for the whole year, vacuum packets of veal and chicken), oil and gas from the mower, the rubber of car and bike tires. Then, in the baffled silence of the door set in its rubber seal, he turned to his wife of forty years and put his hand out and felt along the inside of her fleshy waist, squeezing her into silence (for she had been talking to him the whole way about Drew, Janet's current boyfriend, who had a tattoo on his arm and flew sailplanes in Cancún). He was raising his lips to her lips. The constrictions in his throat were coming again, the muscle there to drive the food down, to make a simple thing like a swallow happen. To get rid of the sensation, he was kissing his wife. The night was silent around them. There were, as one would expect, tears of frustration. There were soft murmurs of love. There was his hand along her spine. And a few minutes later, the automatic door light, on a delayed fuse, popped off, sending them into the ease-ful dark.

THE GRIP

BENEATH HIM the metal gave and sang accompanied by
the tedious clack of rail gaps; it was the couplings whack-
ing each other, or something. Jim didn't know the parts
the way some did, the ones who had worked on the lines;
he was just hanging on, and had been since the yards in
Albuquerque, where he'd clambered up between cars and
then, before he could jump back down, found himself
stuck as the train opened up full throttle and darkness
fell, which it did along this stretch of the Rio fast and
quick, the sun sliding off the emptiness, leaving him with
only his grip and a foothold that wasn't sure. It was very
cold. The heat rose up through the translucent sky, was
gone, and he was left in his cotton shirt—moth-holed and
tattered. (He'd left Ohio in this same damn shirt, the very

same one.) He'd heard stories of men in the same circumstances, men betrayed by bad leaps onto sluggishly moving freights; he'd heard the tall tales of men who held on in poor positions all night, into the next day, and through another weary night until their tendons locked and their muscles broke and they were saved at the last second when the destination was reached or the train pulled to a siding to let an express pass. Then with their arms out like zombies they'd stumble off between the couplings and lay in the grass, scream into the sky. The other side, too, he'd heard. Those who held on for a night and then tried to find some way to climb up to the walk only to fall to a depraved death. The grip he had was a solid one, and there was a toehold below, on a shank of metal coming out of the car, a piece of broken hardware that had no apparent use. The foothold wasn't much, and to keep it he had to rest his weight on the side of his boot, his arch; when that got sore, he moved back to his toes. About fifty minutes into the ride, he slipped off his toes and had to rely on his grip to keep himself from falling. That was when he decided it would be best to keep his arch over the nub. His buddy Roy was farther down, probably on top of a car, and maybe he'd work his way along and, looking down, see him there and somehow conspire to find a way to help him up, maybe making a loop with his belt (did he have a belt?), because Roy had been riding for months and knew the tricks of the trade. Roy had a tight-lipped, know-it-all look. He chewed over his knowledge, his tales of the road, long and hard before talking them out.

This was a long dull stretch of empty land, desert hard and straight, allowing the engineer to open it up so that

the train, despite its enormous length, might sizzle through
the landscape and make the yards in Fe by dawn; he reck-
oned his grip would hold until dawn, to say the least, and
maybe through the next day if he had to do it, because he
knew what had to be done to stay alive in this life. He'd
been called an animal by his adopted aunt, and he found
himself—as he wandered around—drawing strength and
life from the comparison. One day after another it had
been basically by living the life of an animal that he survived (he'd confessed all this to Roy in an apostolic rant by
the campfire one night over a couple of bottles of sour
mash); he figured his grip was tough enough, fingers thick
and hard from the last job he'd had hauling ice in Ohio,
wrists good and thick as the rest of his torso, at least down
to his legs, which were long and thin and rather elegant;
he figured all this would conspire to hold him onto the
car at least to Fe.

Night settled on the train. The trails of light in the
sky, which flickered above him, little feathers of high cir-
rus with orange and magenta hues, were swallowed up by
the purest and finest dark he'd ever known. The dark
seemed to be a thick oil pouring from under the train and
up and over him until—this was an hour or two later—he
wasn't sure how long he'd been there and how long he was
going to have to wait for dawn. He wasn't sure of much
except of the pain in his arch above the nub, and that he'd
had to loosen his grip, flex his fingers, putting even more
weight on that nub before he made the contortion—almost slipping off in the process—to get his weight trans-
ferred to the other foot.

Above him the sparkling display of the cosmos framed

by the lip of the hopper gave testimony to the train's movement, to space and time passing, but he didn't see it. He didn't see the passing of stars; the spiraled celestial movement. He held on and held on tight and time slipped away. Time didn't pass. Or it did pass. He was remembering the time he'd been at the house, in Galva, in the backyard, playing beneath large double sheets on the line as they bloomed and folded with wind like spinnakers, starched by the sun while his mother—making that soft little hum sound she made when she was occupied by herself—put more pins into more cloth, or just stood there with her back to him scrutinizing the horizon, as if in the view his father would appear as an aberration of light; for his father was one of those long-lost salesmen who took to the road selling and rarely came back: a scuff of his hard soles on the kitchen floor, the bootblack smell, his thick ungainly arms were the sole fragments left of the man. That one single moment in the yard reclining against the grass watching his mother, or just listening to her make sound out of air against her teeth and lips; and then, along with that, a memory of her arms giving him one of her great, big bear hugs. That moment seized up and fell away when the great strain of the grip—the flaring pain of it—superseded all memory and he held on for dear life. The fear burned the memory away, like a projector bulb melting a hole in jammed film. What did it matter? It was the last memory of her anyhow, all he had left of it. She died before she could fully reveal herself to him. After her death the rest of his childhood was short-lived and brutal, a series of bleak portraits, fuzzy daguerreotypes of his aunts—he was passed from home to home until his body hard-

ened to adulthood and the Depression set in and he began to drift.

The night took on vast, grand proportions; the night
was liquid and runny, stretched taught until it was no more
than a thin strand of hot white burning his foot and palm.

With great laborious heaves the train slowed and began to lug up the grade into the foothills—but not slow
enough to allow him to jump from his strange position,
twisted partway around so he wasn't able to find the lever-
age for a leap that would clear him from the wheels and
the girth of the car; in any case the energy he'd need for
such a stunt was gone—or so he thought, calculating and
making odds. It was the slow deceleration of the train, the
decreasing clicks of rail links, that broke him from his odd
reverie about his mother (which as far as he knew was the
last real thing he'd thought of aside from his grip, the nub
that was burning hellfire into his foot; maybe a stray
thought of how good a slug of Roy's Ripple would taste at
that very moment). He had no large philosophical map of
the world upon which to consider his situation. His intention, his sole intention, was to live through the night,
to hold on. Far in the dark the train gave a low whistle,
probably to scare off a coyote from the tracks. No God-
fearing soul would find himself this far in the desert, even
with water towers spaced periodically. Again he considered the stories of men who had ventured out into the
desert only to watch the sardonic waves of brakemen and
fellow hobos from the open mouths of passing boxcars; he
considered again the fantastic tall tales of men such as himself, holding on for dear life in stupefying positions for
days on end. Those tales had always sounded preposter-

ous and stupid and impossible to anyone who'd gone through the experience of riding between cars for more than an hour. But those were the best stories, the ones that held the campfire crowd longest, the bullshits and yeah rights just adding to the fun of telling them.

One of two things was going to give: the grip or the toehold. If the grip went—already he'd lost it a bit that one time he was changing feet—he would count on the foothold. If the foothold went he'd hope for the strength to cling with his fingers long enough to regain his footing. The car had a slight rhythmical sway to it. The tracks were set in clean, white ballast, but they weren't perfect. In the time he'd been holding on—an hour, maybe four, most likely not more than that because there wasn't even the slightest trace of dawn-light in the sky—he'd learned the dance she made; his cheek rested against the metal side; he tasted it with his lips, metal and old paint and creosote and ashblack. The dance was the waltz, a three-count thing. Now it was slowing, and he did a shift, putting all the weight on the nub as he switched to his cold, dew-damp left hand and then spun slightly—in congruence with the sway of the car, it seemed—to the other foot.

Again far up in the future there was the thin squeal of the whistle.

The train seemed to be slowing even more, although if there was one thing that he had learned from Roy it was that there was no speed better than a dead stop for departing a train; and any hobo worth shit knew that there was nothing harder than gauging the speed of a train once you were under her spell; men were betrayed by all kinds of things, and one thing that could do you in was thinking the clacks were slowing, that there was a long space between them, when all you'd done is stopped hearing them; stopped listening; or the rails were longer, or it just didn't matter anymore and you were ready to pack it in.

His relationship with oblivion was a tight one. He'd looked out into the long blank stare of the Great Plains for hours on end. He'd lain atop a load of coal clear across the plains of Nebraska and let his eyes swallow the cosmos from one end to the other.

Roy had one of those strange, twisted voices, half yokel but with a hint of some kind of feigned dignity that came from attending a good college out East before Wall Street fell out from under his life. Some said he had a house and two kids and even a little cocker spaniel behind him like so much refuse, trash tossed along the roadway. Others said he'd once been a strong businessman, a compatriot of Rockefeller. In a hobo shack someplace outside of Cleveland a man had whispered into the darkness—secreting his words in soft, husky grunts—that Roy had once played croquet with Lindbergh. Who knew? It was as possible as anything else in the world. So when Roy's voice appeared up over the top edge of the car it seemed both angelic and harsh at the same time; he barked commands over the roar of the train. The commands were grand and oratorical: To jump clear of the tracks, Jim, all you have to do, he said, is find the resolve, the spunk, the go-get-it attitude. It was the voice of a man addressing the Rotary Club about civic pride and boosterism on one hand, and on the other it had undertones of fatherly advice.

Outlined with starlight and what perhaps was the first

fine hints of twilight, he could see Roy's hand up there reaching down to him with a furtive little waving motion. Give me your hand, the voice said firmly. It would be simple. Roy would haul him up and over the side of the car and then they'd have a celebratory smoke, flicking the ash and spark off into the slipstream, not saying a whole hell of a lot but letting the silence itself spread around the fantastic way in which he'd survived the ordeal. He'd wait out asking Roy if he had any sense at all of how long he'd been hanging on with his grip; he'd savor the response that was about to come: two fucking hours, or three, or longer. Then with this information imparted they'd chuckle at the odd ways of the universe and shimmy their way along the top of two cars until they found a hopper in which to dig out rounded spots of coal upon which to catch a bit of shut-eye.

Jim had to persuade himself of the truth, to go about it systematically. The voice he was hearing was nothing more than the constant stream of passing air being twisted by his pain; and the waving hand above coaxing him to let go was nothing but his tired eyes giving way to hope. He'd seen mirages before, fantastically real, opening up over the fields of Iowa and Utah; he'd seen a great lake of pure fresh water amid which there was a raft and girls being towed on skis behind a boat; he'd seen large Indian faces, passive with judgment and wisdom, staring down out of the sage and bramble. To believe in them was one thing, because it was just as possible to believe in a mirage as it was to believe in anything else; but to expect out of a mirage what you'd expect out of something real and tangible was nothing but foolhardiness; many a good hobo had gone that route, put faith in the visions—gone the way of large open lakes with speedboats towing skiers; and died for it. He'd learned that the best visions were the ones you sat back and took in without trusting one bit; on the other side of the coin he'd seen real sights that were as good as mirages because they were so far removed from his trust, his fingers. Once, on the East Coast, on a New York stopover selling pears on the street, he'd taken a train out to the edge of the Bronx, and then a street car farther out until he found himself on the verge of some avenue of great wealth on which the houses, stately and large, were draped by sweeping crowns of maple and oak. It seemed to him to be vestiges of a land so grand and fantastic that he sat down on the sidewalk right there, crossed his legs, and wept with his face cupped in his palms. Then a man came along, a colored gentleman in a wide white shirt and dark blue dungarees, his face as dark as pitch, swollen with years of hard work. He asked if things were right. Then he offered a glass of water, taking him back along a side path to the kitchen door of one place, making him wait there until he came back out with a tall, dark green glass, actual cubes of ice clinking inside it, and made him take a long drink before telling him to get on his way because the likes of him weren't appreciated around those parts. Back on the sidewalk, facing the house again, he'd been uncertain as to the validity of the event. Had he gone with the Negro to the back door to have his thirst quenched? Or was he just working into the scene his own form of indulgence, spurred on by the thirst he was feeling? Sitting on that sidewalk his throat was as parched as it had been on any of his travels across the desert, not even a small trace of spittle available to relieve the clench of his esophagus or the dry paper of his tongue; and now on the train with his grip failing he was just as thirsty. But he was awake. That much was sure. He was as awake as he'd ever be. He made a little shift of his foot—now so numbed he was hardly able to call it his own—and tried to flex his fingers without letting go, and instead he did let go and the full brunt of his body was on the nub for a second and then his foot slipped completely off and just in time—in conjunction with another heartfelt wail of the horn far up—he regained his handhold.

There were only two endings to the tall tales traded before their beleaguered campfires: men fell to their death, or they lived on gallantly against odds that were as wide as the sky and as twisted as Joshua trees. Well fuck all that, he said, cursing his slip, the closeness to which he'd come to being eaten by the wheels. Fuck all this. It was time to let go or be let go of, one way or another. It was time that the long snaking oblivion of the night—the ceaseless clank and rattle of the couplings below, the scene of desert at night—of juniper and dust and dew combined—had its will.

But he did not let go with an attempted jump, and the reason was simple and left him until the late fifties when he was on his deathbed in Toledo, Ohio, with his son Carter by his side, holding his hand, and he remembered it again. Down at the camp by the water tower, right before falling into the deepest sleep of his life, he vowed to himself not to forget it, and he told Roy to remember what he was going to say, and to repeat it to him when he woke. Don't let me forget that, he said, for Jesus' sake when I get up and I'm myself again tell the whole story to remind me. He'd staggered a few yards up the track where the switchman told him to go. He'd never forget the kindly switchman who saw him stumble out from between cars and fall to his knees. Dressed in railroad overalls, an oil can in one hand, the switchman came over and helped him to his feet and asked him if he was all right. Here's a nickel because you didn't ask for one, he said, passing it over, shaking his head in a bemused but respectful manner when he saw where the kid had held on—the small handle, the bit of metal sticking out below—clear across the desert.

Right above the lip of the car, in that open starlit space that was only a slight variation of darkness—only a tiny bit lighter than the train itself—he saw her small, pure face, like some kind of ripe fruit; in it he saw his own eyes, marled brown with flecks of mica, and the shape of his own mouth, thin and tight around the teeth. So sure was he that this wasn't an aberration, that this was in no way a mirage, that he called out her name several times. Mom. Mom. Mom. She reached down to him, her arms long and thin and frail-looking in the darkness; she reached down to him and put her fingers around his fingers and held them tightly there—grip holding forearm; grip holding forearm—until twilight began to merge with the dark and spread above the train.

My own mother's fingers appeared, he told Roy, who looked away with skeptical shame over his companion's confession; it was a sad sight to see his buddy sink to this point without him being drunk out of his mind on Ripple. Promise me you'll tell me. I forget everything in my sleep, he said. Ah shit, I'll tell you, Roy muttered, spitting once into the weeds.

For all it matters to the world he might as well have been eaten by the wheels, another dead body kicked free of his grip by bad luck, weakness, ill timing, or a sadistic railroad bull. There were plenty of dead in that time of wandering. He shared the story with his son shortly before he passed away in Toledo's Flower Memorial Hospital, where his son was a resident radiologist. He had seen his mother's face up there, real and pure, as hard as carved stone. And he'd lived to speak of it to his son, who wept to see his father's x-rays reveal the cloudy result of seventy years of Lucky Strikes. Your grandmother's fingers were surprisingly strong, he said. They wrapped around mine and together we worked our way out of the night and into the next morning when, like a song of mercy, the clacks slowed and the train came off the long grade and stopped to take on water.

Then he told his son about Roy, and how he'd made him promise to repeat the tale to him when he awoke, and how after making that request he fell face down into the brambles and slipped into the deepest sleep of his life.

WHAT
I HOPE FOR

I DON'T want anyone to die in my stories anymore. From here on out it has to be a glorious life. The light in the late evening from the ferry to the island will glimmer and pop off the horizon, the last of the sun going down; they'll lean on the rail, shoulder to shoulder, feeling the soft heave of the boat, knowing that once they arrive at the bed and breakfast—the little sachet of potpourri dangling from the closet rack, and a mint on the pillow—they'll undress to behold each other in naked splendor. The next day they'll rent bikes and ride into the headwinds until their thighs (they never ride at home, in the city) are tight; they'll picnic far out, on the end of the island, in a cove protected from the wind. Only an occasional gust will grit their potato salad. There they'll kiss slowly and he'll lick the salt from her lips and marvel at the warmth of her mouth in contrast to the hard cold outside, over the cove, where the surf roars in. On the way back, with the wind behind them, they'll feel the exhilaration of a jet going with the jetstream; they'll spread their arms outward, spinnakers to capture the wind. Parking their bikes under the porch, locking the chains, they'll wobble up to the lobby on weak legs. Oh so tired, they'll be, so wonderfully weak-kneed, as if navigating on land for the first time in years; and in this anguish of exhaustion they'll make love again upstairs, half dressed, and then fall asleep through the dinner hour, only to rise in the darkness with the shudder of the storm outside, and with that barely perceptible awareness that something had been missed, something of the utmost importance. In the hall, the door is creaking and the man across the way, who they presume is a loner, is wending his way to the bathroom (which they share), and they both listen, holding their breath to hear the sound of his pee in the water, which no longer makes them laugh the way it did the first time they heard it, in the morning, but now sounds like something that *has* to be done, cold firm water against water in a porcelain bowl. If no one dies in the story, this is how it will be: the two of them a day later getting back on the boat and returning to the mainland, watching the landscape slip behind the boat, the gulls dashing above the wake, and the wake itself smoothing out from the v, fading off into the eternal uproar of the North Atlantic.

THE
INTERRUPTION

THEY STAYED together on the coldest night of the year,
wondering when the security guys might find it in themselves to come out, to send them on their way—and there
were ways to be taken even on a winter night, paths that
might be taken depending on which guy stumbled first in
which direction. Arno had his arm up around the back of
Roy's shoulder as he hunched close to the old man and tried
to hear what he was saying—a prattle partly drowned out
by the knit cap over his own ears, and partly by a vibration from beneath their frozen boots, coming from the air
circulation systems of the Hilton, a low drab noise that
was part of the attraction of the spot, like the lowest note
on a cathedral organ; Arno listened, half concerned for
what Roy was plotting and half concerned for the split in

his lip which had opened up and seemed to carry within a chasm of pain too wide for such a small crack in his flesh.

"You go in," the old guy was sputtering, "and say you have a meeting to attend to and then just slip on past that desk they have there and act like you know where you're going and find the biggest frickin' party going on . . . then just slink your cold ass back out here to us with what you get . . . We'll feast like kings . . . "

Three bitter cold nights had clamped down on the men, moved them from one locale to another but never into any kind of sustained warmth; a few minutes in the entryway to an apartment building before they were moved on; a few hours in the public library hiding behind opened copies of the *Elma Gazette;* five minutes inside the vestibule of the First National Bank leaning against the long slab of marble, knees half bent in an effort to ease the shudder of their tired legs, but not sitting down, because to sit would be an admission of needing the full hold of gravity and that, in itself, would draw the attention of the proprietors. All over town it was the proprietors who came and asked them, sometimes kindly and sometimes not, to move on.

"Go on, Arno, give it a shot," Snag said. Snag was sixteen or seventeen, with the face of a seventy-five-year-old beach bum. He had long hair that was clumped together with scalp oil, real oil, dirt and old vomit—what was left over from the old dreadlock thing he used to have. His eyes, if looked at long enough, solidified into something along the lines of ice cubes; in them one found the stiff coldness that comes from all the drugs, combined with the beatings his old man had given him. His arms were long and thin and brittle with track marks. If asked, he says he doesn't use drugs. Never has. And there is something about his story—the wide claims he makes—that rings true with the other guys. He hasn't used drugs. If anything, the needles have shot *him* up. The crack had to burn someplace, and it picked *his* pipe. All the monkeys pounding randomly on typewriters ended up writing *his* story.

"Why don't you do it, Snag? Go in the fuckin' hotel." Arno barely opened his lips over his damaged teeth. Plumes of ice-smoke illustrated his words. He isn't a big fan of this kid. Having a kid like this around can get you into trouble. Snag wasn't from Elma. He had an outsider's skewed vision—from Dearborn, near Detroit.

"We can get past the high school kid," Snag persisted. "All you have to do is get Roy over there"—he turned, nodded past the bright yellow-copper lights to another hunk of decorative bush—"and let him start pissing or something so the guy comes out. He comes out to yell at Roy, we go in. Simple as that."

There was a long communal silence as the men thought over the situation. Zeek began nodding yes to some unspoken question and kept it up for a long time. Zeek was fifty, soft in the head, with a clot of beard around his mouth that gave him the alternative nickname Lint Trap. (He'd die in a few weeks of a bleeding ulcer—half his blood would end up in his stomach cavity, swishing around while his blood pressure dipped. A ten-year-old boy, delivering his Sunday morning papers, would find him frozen to death.)

No one remembers how long it was before Roy, in a sudden burst of what might be called the inspiration of the last ditch, stood up and stretched his arms over his head. His pants were tattered, moth-holed, picked up at Goodwill years ago. "Ah, shit, I'm gonna do it myself," he said, and before Arno or anyone else could respond, he was off into that semicircle of brightly lit concrete, moving swiftly, parting the electric doors while the valet bent down to adjust his radio, or tie his combat boots—not that it mattered. The men didn't show the slightest interest in following their friend into that bright abyss. They sat back down, closing the circle, holding their own in a silent huddle, shaking their heads slightly, while Arno remembered how remarkable the bow in the old fart's legs had been as he stood under the steaming water in the shower at the First Baptist shelter; they were thin legs that bowed under the weight of a long, hard life.

The din in the room hissed with the dull undercurrents of a second marriage; the dark ceiling hung with long strands of crimped silver foil. Below the silver strands were twenty round tables. At one of them Mr. Standard worked on his third Scotch, barely able to hold the plastic cup in his large hands. He wanted to crush the cup, to watch it explode. The reception—after about an hour of bad toasts—had become as flat and dull as a bad ball game; nothing was moving, just a shimmer of heat over a blank field. On the dais along with the rest of the wedding party sat Melville, Mel Horton, the groom, with his frank, round face that seemed—at least to Standard—to need breaking in, like a new baseball glove. Someone should pour neat's-foot oil onto it and mash a fist around, grind it right in— get that rich freshness, that silver-spoon suck, out of those cheeks, he thought. But then he looked over at his wife, at her narrow cheekbones and the fine shape of her wrists. She certainly wouldn't approve of such a thought one bit. She was best friends with the bride, Susan Porter, who was up there now, shifting around in her wedding gown with that sad complacency Standard had seen a hundred times in other second-timers. He was a firm believer in the downfall of man. His company, Standard Pipe, was going through harder times, having traveled through hard times. It was rusting out, literally: long bleeding smears of rust drew tongues along the patched corrugated steel sides of the main works. Windows were broken and he was barely able to mill his orders anymore. As he sucked his Scotch he kept thinking about Melville Horton's last visit to the office. The bastard stood there in that fine suit of his with his hands dug deep into his pockets. Standard's office was a little backroom deal, with yellowed blinds and overstuffed filing cabinets and no pretensions of grandeur. On the wall to the left were his old Rotary Club plaques, a few golf trophies blued by dust. One drawer of the file cabinet was open, off the track, and had been that way for ten years. Strangely, this office didn't in any way really reveal the true nature of Standard, who, by most measures, was fastidious and careful in both his personal matters and his business matters. His cuticles were groomed, his nails perfectly clipped. The office just didn't matter to him much, not the way the actual metalworks did. And so when Melville Horton sniffed and ran a thumb over his Rotary Man of the Year 1968 plaque, he felt the kind of deep sense of imbalance that just about sent him into a sputtering rage; if there was anything he hated more in the world, it was being snubbed by a kid who wasn't even a sperm cell when he was wading ashore at Normandy.

"I can't do this kind of business," Horton was saying, moving back from the plaque, looking for a chair, finding an old one with a green seat, cross-hatched with gray duct tape. He remained standing. "How am I supposed to get my orders filled when this stuff you're supposed to do isn't there in time? I've got a machinist rigging a whole new getup, and Bob is working overtime to get the old one running, and then I'm told by Standard that there isn't pipe coming—so all that work's for naught."

Standard looked him up and down before he spoke. Horton was young enough to be his son, the one killed near Khe Sanh, Hill 861, as a member of the 1/9. But unlike his son, who had been tough, a prime all-state quarterback in high school, this kid had a yuppie gloss. His suit was cut a bit too big, hanging over his fat stomach, loose and bagging on the shoulders. "The order's coming," Standard mumbled. "I said it would, and it will. We're just overbooked. I mean Tilco went nuts. Sent us double widths accidentally. Then this train strike, I mean, to get a box order from Dayton took me a month; and then the fucking thing derailed."

This kid Melville Horton didn't understand the old-fashioned unspoken agreement that you didn't march into a man's office during a train strike demanding a late job if it wasn't a matter of real cash. He was an idiot. And Melville wasn't short on money, not with his shop taking a hundred orders a week. On top of that he was operating the whole thing as a kind of hobby anyhow, because his old man's old man had founded Cap Soaps before it was incorporated. The bastard cashed in when it went public.

He had plenty of liquid assets to move around when needed. The kid didn't have to worry about derailments or bad tooling. The jerkoff could buy the frickin' railroad if he felt like it.

The DJ was playing mambo music. There was a muffled announcement, another last-ditch toast to pump life into the reception. Standard put the plastic cup to his lip and sucked the last drops out of the ice.

"Honey." Ellen Standard put her hand over his. She knew and wanted to ease his thirst. His third was gone and already he was starting to get up. Susan was coming, making the rounds, raising the skirt of her wedding dress as she walked to reveal her thick ankles. She'd gained more weight during the engagement than during the last ten years, since her last marriage.

"I'm getting a refill," he said, trying to sound casual. There was an edge of panic in his voice, as if the bar might close.

"Congrats, Susan," he said, barely stopping, just brushing her arm with his and then heading off, swaying slightly, into the dark. There were three people dancing to "Flashdance," doing a feeble, half-remembered disco step. The music was loud against the hard walls. It boomed from the speakers, black boxes that went halfway to the ceiling. The DJ worked his CD player with amazing seriousness, like a judge presiding over a trial. His face was firm, and he spent time between songs making marks on a clipboard. It was a sad, lonely job, providing music for occasions like this. But on this night, watching Frank Standard sway over to the bar for the fourth time—noting the solemn way the man held his eyes fixed on the bartender—

the DJ had a premonition: he felt a shift in the evening, and he would later say that he knew this reception was doomed to some traumatic event. If anyone in the world could feel it coming, he could. He was an expert on the tedium of modern rituals; on the watered-down inability most wedding receptions had of rising above their own careful, deliberate cheerlessness. So when Roy walked through the double doors, smelling of the shit that had dripped down his leg as he swaggered quickly through the hotel lobby, past two guards who were talking heatedly about the Pistons game, the DJ wasn't surprised: he just lowered the volume dial from ten to seven and sat back.

Two years later, when the divorce papers were signed by both parties, it would be the interruption that people would remember if they thought of the reception at all; the way Roy stood beneath the frame of the doorway, legs apart, arms out from his sides slightly, reeking so much that even the Hilton's ventilation system, roaring air up through five-foot-wide vents, couldn't compete; shit and urine and sweat and body odors along with the reek of bourbon on his breath and a hint of garlic from a slice of pizza he'd dug out of a dumpster that afternoon for lunch. It was one of those smells that remain indelible, scratched in the stone of dendrites, a smell that says we're all from shit, nothing more or less, God forgive us. And it's this smell that Susan Horton, who after two years had taken on certain refinements of class, thought of as she sat on the deck of the house looking out over the Mediterranean. She was thinner. She'd lost twenty-odd pounds since she arrived at the house, which sat on a cliff, fifty miles from

Málaga. Around it, desert stretched; it was Africa, really, licking that edge of Spain, she'd been told by Peter, the Brit who took care of the American houses during the off-season. He picked her up at the airport in Almería. A squat man with a large forehead. He'd been a British paratrooper, he explained, lifting the cuff of his shirt to show an old tattoo, so faded and blotched it was more like a birthmark. The deck was made of smooth flagstones, with small pebbles between, and felt good on the feet when you returned from the beach. She went down to the water every day, after lunch, stayed for two hours, alone on her straw mat, reading the salty paperbacks someone had left behind, and then, returning alone to the deck, she had a gin and tonic and looked from her spot in the shade out over the landscape. This afternoon, the odor returned to mind. She hadn't seen Roy when he first staggered into the reception. A description of his entrance came to her via Horton's sister, Edith, who spoke of it later that evening when the celebration was over, when Roy, beaten black and blue, was sleeping soundly in the county holding cell. The room was cleared of guests, except for the bride and groom, Edith, Ronald, her husband, and Ellen Standard, who was trying to patch up her husband's reputation. The room was bright, revealing the pipes overhead and the beleaguered black walls marred with kick marks and gouges from high school proms. Under the lights it was impossible to miss the wide oval stain where Roy had deposited his vomit first, before anybody really got to him, before the kicking began. Edith told her that part; she spoke of it as one might of a delicious appetizer. *It was truly grotesque. That, that man, he just stood there. I couldn't believe my eyes.*

Good god the smell was just perfectly awful. By the fruit and salad bar, bowls set tight in chipped ice; that's what he moved towards, with Standard and the DJ and a few others the first to notice.

Two weeks after the wedding, the night Roy died with Arno attending to his needs, the first hairline fracture appeared in her marriage—at least in hindsight it looked that way. She sipped the gin and tonic, rattled the ice, felt the cool air from the surface of the drink and thought about it: they'd gone to Wal-Mart on a lark, to buy some Christmas lights, to slum it a bit, parking his Ferrari in the hinterlands to avoid runaway carts, getting out under the sodium lights, finding a strange excitement in the bleak span of pavement. It was snowing quite hard, sticking in clumps to her fur stole. Around the front entryway to the store a few vagabonds lingered. (At the time, the word vagabond fit her vision of these hovering shadows edging around the periphery of things. Her father, a hardworking Hungarian immigrant, looked upon bums as unclean, and he couldn't help instilling in his only daughter the view that such people were simply wandering out of their own accord, stray hunks of humanity who had lost a toehold on the earth. She had memories of the homeless camp on the edge of Elma one particularly bad year; these were, mostly, men who came down from Canada to pick blueberries, living in an array of makeshift canvas tarps, tents, lean-tos. You could smell it for miles, her father claimed. Dirty people. She was seven years old, and a man came to the house for a cup of water or coffee. In Spain, on the mesa, she had a brief vision of him: his beautiful eyes, marbled brown, in a young face. He was a boy, really. He was her age, a young boy. He had his thumbs tucked into the pockets of his dungarees. She kissed him for no reason. She just felt like it and did it and then there was her father shouting in Hungarian, as he did when he got so angry his circuits shorted out and English was superseded by his native tongue. He chased the boy a half mile and gave him a lashing with a small shank of pine furring strip. This was after the war, after the Depression and during a strange readjustment when the protocol for approaching such people was being transformed; the country, exploding with riches, no longer had even the smallest room for the dirty, not even a brush with them, she thought, now, on the deck, listening to the gardener moaning slightly to himself.) Inside the store that night there was the stunning, opulent glare of neon racked upon neon, the warmth of aisles stuffed with products—and feeling giddy, they went to the section where the Christmas decorations were. Immediately they began to argue. The argument developed into a fight. The fight was over which kind of lights, white or colored, would look best woven around the front banisters—that's all she could remember, holding the glass back and letting a piece of ice rest against her front teeth until the cold permeated to the soft center. The sun was behind the mountains, and the dusty, rubble-specked landscape became bathed in the orange afterlife of a day; black swifts dove past the whitewashed houses. Somewhere out of sight the gardener was sloshing water into the flower beds. It was the constriction of their words she could recall; the tone of it; the passing of information in clipped phrases—for what should have been a warm, soft choice—

a romantic choice; it was her first indication of the resolute stodginess that went all the way through Horton
Melville. She smiles and thinks of the British man, Peter,
asking her to go for a drink; she remembers his bulk, un-
stable on large legs, the way he bounced on the balls of his
feet like a kid. Was it love she felt for this man, his ruddy
face, cut square, his lingering Cockney accent; his British
paratrooper tattoos? She was no longer the kind of woman
who would avoid feeling intensely about someone after
only a few meetings, she told herself; her experiences with
Horton had settled into her view of life, and she was now
quite sure that one was best guided by first impulses, by
spur-of-the-moment movements, not by some obligation
to long-winded common sense.

Arno held on to Roy and guided him along the back of
the train station, which stood dark before rails of bleeding
rust. One train a day came through to pick up passengers
and go on to Detroit, crawling so slowly it didn't polish
the rust away. They were heading towards the old B.+O.
control tower, a wobbling tinderbox, half burned along
one side by someone's out-of-control campfire; behind it
was an old wax paper factory, every window broken out,
gaping at the snow-filled sky. (This was around the time
Horton, inside Wal-Mart, held up a set of white lights
and said, tightly, "I'd rather maintain tradition.") And
behind *them,* fifty yards, near the graded road crossing,
was a red spot in the snow where Roy had vomited, folded
over like an empty wallet while Arno held him around the
waist, feeling only the hard bones, nothing left in the way
of legs.

"Fucking hold on, Roy," Arno said.

"We'll make it, old man," Roy said.

"Shit's a foot deep if it's two."

"Yep."

Roy didn't want to die; and Arno was busting ass to keep him moving. Snow was falling lightly. Everything had a five-inch coat. There was nothing—to Roy's mind— like the silence of a snowy night, especially in the worst parts of town where, out of their own dilapidation, hulks of the past took on a particular beauty. He loved that. Many winters he'd huddled in the B.+O. tower with his fellows, taking sips, smoking, listening to nothing at all except, perhaps, the keen buzzing isolation of his own loneliness. The tower was a good place to be, and he wanted to be there. It was high up. No matter how often the railroad boarded over the windows, a crew of homeless folks took it upon themselves to shove the plywood sheets away. Under a pile of newsprint, in a corner, you could usually find warmth enough to hold you until daylight. But his busted gut was sending shooting pain across his rib cage. The autopsy would reveal a bruised spleen. His own memory of events had been culled by drink, anyway. If one were to compile all that Roy could fully remember on this snowy night, one might have an oblong collection of images: cold wooden floors; windows with holes stuffed with yellowed paper, the paper mill across the street where his old man used to work; the way men sat on the windowsills in the summer, holding their lunch boxes, eating; the long gaunt features of his mother's face twisting when she was hit, the vacant recesses of her eyes, beady and black. Nights on the streets removed many memories completely. His life now subsisted on a small kernel at the very center of his mind, and that kernel was the side of his father's wide palm striking him one morning when he was about eight, breaking his jaw so that it hung as limp as laundry from the line . . . and that was enough to fuel him on this snowy night.

The gardener was extremely thin, his dark blue work pants limp from his legs, and the hose quivered in his hand. Her gin and tonic was finished, and she was sitting, watching the light fade away from the rubble, the sea glistening, listening to voices rising up from the beach below. She wasn't sure of his name—Miguel was her guess. He was hired by Peter, and Peter did most of the talking to him.

"*Hola,*" she said.

He grunted, lifted the hose a bit too high, splashed water on his toes. He lay the hose at the base of a bush and took a bandanna from his pocket to wipe his shoes. They were the kind of shoes she saw for sale at the market: truck-tire treads, cheap, thin, suede leather. She'd gone to the market that morning, accompanied by Peter, who said it was part of his job to drive visitors—ones who didn't have rented cars—to Carbonaras. The intense dryness of the country along with the unexpected relentlessness of the morning heat seemed to kick her olfactory nerves into high gear. Suddenly everything had a precise smell: The dust. Sand. The rocks around the houses. The buckets of cheap, plastic housewares. Rows of detergent bottles. Long tables of leather goods; and of course the fish and bread. On the deck, watching Miguel slosh water around the other bushes (if she had looked carefully she would have seen how he plied the hose with great respect, sloshing but only in a certain jittery way. The scarcity of water was a part of his bones, his dry, brittle skin; from the wells it came saline and rank), she touched the side of her arm near her elbow where Peter, in the crush of the crowd, had held her, guided her like a blind woman.

From the B.+O. tower switch room there was a view of the cantilevered arches holding up the snow-covered roof of the unused train station. Along one wall of the building stood an old luggage cart with metal wheels, the only thing that hadn't been destroyed, vandalized, painted over with tags, defiled by piss or shit or broken glass because it was too large—and the wheels were frozen in place with rust— to shove off the platform. In the tower a long tongue of snow had drifted in through the missing window and forced them back against the rear wall, where they sat, legs up, huddled against each other. Roy's breathing was labored and deep. His face was rough with unshaven hair. He seemed to work his mouth around each breath. Arno lit a Camel, took a draw, held it to his friend's mouth.

"Come on, you old fuck. Hang on."

(Hang on. To what? For what? Arno had not the slightest idea how or what the old fuck was supposed to hang on to. For his death was so much writing on the wall, a certitude against which no bets would be placed. His statement here was perhaps just a lulling platitude spoken out of a sense of duty to those conditions of death. In that case it might be said that Arno had risen to the highest condition of humanity in that he was playing out his role upon the stage, the penultimate stage, of the end of his friend's life. On the other hand, maybe Arno meant it; maybe he simply wanted Roy to hang on to life, nothing more, or less. Perhaps his idea of dragging Roy to the B.+O. tower was to find at least a small bit of domesticity; four walls, perhaps a blanket of old *Elma Gazettes*, maybe a jackpot bottle of port; better yet, maybe they'd get arrested and find contentment in jail.)

At least they'd made a night of it, dragging themselves all the way down Main in the snow before stumbling upon Zeek, who was up against the inside corner of a white-scratched Plexiglas bus shelter smoking a tiny, reed-thin, crack-laced joint, jittery with cold and stretched nerves. Inside the shelter, headlights bled like long sizzling lines of melting ice across the milky Plexiglas. The men had a powwow, snorting the cold air, gulping from the neck of a bottle of Boone's Farm cherry wine Zeek had stolen from another wino at knifepoint. When that was gone, Zeek materialized—actually saying the word abracadabra—from behind Roy's head a bottle of Thunderbird, and, opening it, put it to Roy's lips and let him tilt his head back for as long as he wanted. He fed Roy the wine the way you'd feed a baby. Burping the old fuck; making sure he wasn't getting too much air. And even though he was stoned numb, he still got the faint pleasure of seeing the old guy's blood nourished.

Perhaps it is the nature of some weddings to have as their undercurrent the possibility of great violence and tragedy; perhaps that alone is what we hear buzzing beneath the music, the silent movement of balloons and tossed confetti over the hiss of starched gowns, the embrace of tight

collars and cummerbunds. The DJ knew this. He under-
stood it well.

Coming back from the bar with another Scotch, Standard considered the stale business atmosphere of Elma,
the depleted economic resources of that part of the state,
and a recent study indicating a severe shortage of piping
material and rising prices because of Islamic wars in regions of the globe he was hard-pressed to locate on a map.
He felt ready for some shift in the world. The music was
easing. There was a sudden lull. A chunk of the general
chatter was gone, and many people—standing and sitting—seemed to shift course, like a flock of geese changing direction in midflight. Just before he turned to see
Roy staggering in the doorway, he recalled Melville going
down the rickety stairs of his office, shoulders straight,
braced by the pin-striped suit. The Standard Piping sign, wind-
blistered, in need of repair, hung limp in the background.
He'd given a halfhearted lift of his fist to the kid, wanting to
yell something out but knowing that things have changed
and that the Melvilles of the world have prevailed. It isn't
any use. He went back into the office and sat down on his
duct-taped chair and thought about it—not exactly seething, but nursing the tight anger that he kept inside him all
the way through the summer and into the winter, feeling
it as he stepped from his Lincoln Towncar into the cold,
across the lobby of the hotel and into his fourth (or was it
fifth?) Scotch. So when he turned and saw Roy, the deep
wrinkles dwelling on the homeless man's face, the old navy
watch cap politely in his hand, he felt a sharp pleasure at
knowing there was going to be a general ruckus. The stench,
the shit smell, was already drifting around.

..

There is a stillness that only the destitute know. And Arno felt it keenly, helping Roy get comfortable, tucking the folds of his old army coat around the man's skull. He went out to the stairs to smoke—not out of respect or politeness but as an excuse to get out. It had been four months since summer, when nights were easy and they went to the woods outside of town and sat around the scrapwood campfire near Roy's wigwam, enjoying the fruits of a day scavenging dumpsters. The smoke from his Camel conjoined with that of his breath as he blew it out. It was well below zero. The cloud of smoke and breath seemed to stand still. Fuck, he said softly, fuck fuck fuck, flicking the butt out into the darkness.

Around the moment when Roy died, Susan Porter-Horton was brushing her teeth, still adjusting herself to the height of the sink in their new house. The gooseneck faucet plated in real gold got in her way when she washed her face. She made a note to herself that she would have the faucets replaced as soon as things settled in; she'd wait until the pretenses of those first few weeks of being married were over and she was secure enough to make suggestions of that sort. The long, rambling split-level with postmodern flourishes had been built for Melville's first wife. It was full of ghosts from the past. Vows weren't simply washed away even by legal procedures, divorce lawyers or hate. She rinsed her toothbrush and slipped it back into the gold-plated holder, and stared at her face, flabby cheeks, pale, bloodless lips and eyes she didn't trust anymore.

..

(In Spain, after making love to Peter, she lies in bed listening to the wind, arriving hot from the coast of Africa, draw through the windows; she then for a moment, a fleeting moment, goes over a long list of changes she made in the house—she thinks of the faucets, their elegant arches, the fine bone handles, and wonders if she'd have them back now. She gets up, silently, moves across the cool floor. On the bed the large bulk of the ex-paratrooper heaves and sighs, floating amid his own dreams.)

Every gesture becomes grand around death. Arno went back inside and saw that Roy was shivering violently. At a loss for what to do, he did what came naturally and, parting his shirt, lay atop the old guy, holding his weight on his knees and his elbows so he wouldn't crush his ribs; he held this position for as long as he could until he slid down and their stubbled cheeks touched. (They'd shaved a week ago at the Baptist mission, side by side, Arno helping out, drawing the Good News razor along the sunken cheeks of his friend—swishing it in the hot water. There had been a sense then in the air of the impending death when, in the shower, Roy's knees weakened and he slid down to the tiles under the steam. There was none of the slaphappy towel play that had—a year ago—accompanied the early stages of the love between the men, just after they swore over that bottle together. Arno showered alone, while Roy, dried off and dressed, talked to Grant, the pastor. He showered alone so he could masturbate, sliding the bulk of a bar of Irish Spring up and down the sides of his cock—no shame whatsoever coming from the sweet act. The love of his hands for his cock was as pure as any form of love available. It was clean, godly love in the land of the lonely. It took five minutes. The water was warm to hot depending on the use of water in the soup kitchen where the volunteer ladies were rinsing the glasses as they came in. He was thinking soft, lovely thoughts. He was thinking about a girl he knew when he was in tenth grade named Wendy.) Ten minutes later he left Roy's body to freeze.

The men outside the Hilton waiting for Roy to come out that night did so the way anybody would wait for a savior. They sat dreamily considering what was about to transpire: he'd come out brashly with a shit-eating grin and his arms loaded with booty, snaking past the high school kid in the uniform, swaggering his hips in a drunkard's dance of victory while they hooted and hollered. It was their way. They knew how to celebrate the small victories. The men with the arduous determination of stoics. Now and then, after a while, one of them muttered: "I wonder what happened to the old fuck." And another said: "Oh give the old shit a chance, he'll be out. I'm sure he will. For Jesus fuck's sake. Give the guy a chance."† But there was no such Second Coming, of course, and all that kept coming that night and the next was the snow. It fell in great clumps. It fell in a fine powder. It fell in an edgy sleet.

† One is tempted to leave it at that, to end it here with the men sitting hopefully atop the steam grate, the murmur of the hotel ventilation system under them. The snow is still falling over the streets and through the slush the cars push while the general misery of the world seems, for a moment, suspended. But to leave it here would be

to leave the men in their state of blatant hope, like kids waiting for a treat, so full of hope their stomping feet patter and you hear in Zeek's "come on where is he" a mantra to hope lost in the past. So I'll add here the fact that the sliding doors opened and two men escorted Roy out, holding him by the lapels, not kicking him out the door but dragging him along like an old wounded Civil War soldier. He was grunting. There was a dabble of blood on his lip. His side—beneath his coat—was bruised. The interruption had lasted only a few moments. Standard had kicked him several times before Melville and two other men stepped in to pull him back. A few seconds later, maybe half a minute, people went back to their tables, and slowly, gradually, the din began again and the DJ turned the dial up to 9, playing a slow tune because that was what most people wanted to dance to anyway. People feared fast movement. They wanted to make slow, lazy circles out of their lives, tiny depleted steps. All around the room couples gathered each other up and went to the floor to make feeble half circles around the song, marking the territory of their limited expectations. It was a song by the Carpenters. Karen Carpenter had died an early death of anorexia, and most of the people at the wedding, hearing her words, thought of her skinny, ravished body, all the beauty sucked away. It was "Close to You," and it had lyrics with birds and the day of someone's birth and everything else you could want emitted by her full-throated voice. There were days of loneliness and isolation in that voice—fright and fear and a mingling of hope that, corny as the lyrics were, made everyone—Melville, his wife, the whole party—forget the interruption, wash it away until it slowly eased back into the story and became, eventually, so far as I know, part of the general outline of gossip.

THE
WIDOW PREDICAMENT

THE HANDSHAKE with Hugh Lawson turned into a soft wrestling match, a quiet force of fingers against each other along with the soft pumping motion the act required. Outside, the wind-swept rain drew itself into a lull, opening a place into which the people could depart. He leaned close to her, not too close but close enough so he could lower his voice into an intimate whisper—*"I'm sorry for your loss."* She in turn said what every widow has to say to such sympathy, what she'd been saying for weeks on end to all kinds of words and advice, over tuna casseroles and cups of coffee, looking out her kitchen window (because that's where most of the post-death rituals took place) at the long procession of the Hudson River moving through the first few weeks of November. *"It's all right,"* she said, still with his hand in hers because the whole thing really only took a second—a pause before someone said it's stopping, and another batch of people went out the door into the cool air. *"I'm fine."*

They made the video on the last day of their honeymoon, at a hotel in Madrid, a grand four-star place with a glossy, empty, modern lobby and stairs that were too deep for her feet; the width of the stairs would remain with her forever, as would the white marble floor, the wood-polish smell of the elevator, and the porter who smiled nicely when he found out it was their honeymoon and told them, in beautiful, slow, Andalusian Spanish, not to have children right way, to hold off on all of that at least a year— granting them a wide, graceful smile full of white teeth.

Bled back onto the screen: shadows; bad lighting. The play of flesh and electronic failures along with the feeble light from the drawn curtains catching half dusk; it was around nine, which in Madrid in the summer seemed pretty much daytime. The curtains opened onto a bland view, the drive-up to the entry of the hotel, the street—busy with traffic— paled with that dry dusty sepia of a hot day, and lined with diseased trees. Resting on the dressing table, propped up on a couple of books, the camera framed the bed, leaving the invention of their lovemaking only to that particular square of poorly lit space and making it all seem—a week later when they watched it at home in New York—minute, static, dissolved in fuzz. The angles weren't right. They were fucking in a normal manner. Seeing it later, they'd realized that porn flicks were distortions on a number of fronts: acrobatic, oddly real-looking unnatural positions provided visible mechanics of pump and thrust. Pornography was often more natural-looking than the real thing.

Two shapeshifters, godless ghosts. Ron hung over her like a long slab of pale moonlit flesh while beneath him, hardly visible, she lay restive, her outstretched hand opening and closing slowly, grasping air. It was this clawing of air that made her cheeks burn with shame when they viewed the tape together; when she saw that hand, waving like a child from the deck of a departing ship, the beauty of the moment became tarnished forever. It no longer belonged to the realm of memory.

He hovered over her with his arms out as she rolled onto her back. Then he made love to her while his ass, pale as a harvest moon, came in and out of focus. They'd laughed at that, the way the recording continued after they were finished, laying back on the tangled bedsheets— spooning each other. When she stood up, her scarless belly passed and moved away, out of sight. He got up, too, showing the flatness of his ass as he turned, bright as chalk, delineated by his dark tan, ripe from three weeks in the sun, reminding them both of those classic sad rear-end shots of concentration camp survivors, of the row of humiliated prisoners lined up in the Attica Prison courtyard after the riots were over.

Along the road to Fuente Vaqueros there were cork trees. He pointed them out, long and thin, bent back by the wind. Behind the bus a swirl of dust rose. They visited Lorca's birthplace. Cool tile floors. The bed where he was rocked. He signed the book—Ron Stanford. Poet. (Soundmixer.)

..

The river gathers ripples of white—headlights passing over the bridge, beneath the beaded bulbs on the higher reaches. Points along the Westchester shore—parking lots at train stations, house windows, street lamps. It would be precise to say the night is pressing against the windows; there is a soft shudder of giving frames as the wind comes in hard gusts—a cold front, the news said, bringing with it what will certainly be the first snow of the year. Already Buffalo— gulping the moisture of Lake Erie—has ten inches. In a chair, legs curled beneath her, she reads Chekhov in a hard-cover edition Ron purchased a month before he got the news. After that he put the book of stories aside: they don't make sense when I try, he kept saying, and anyway I never liked Chekhov much because he's too dry, too vestal. The only stories that counted were the messages from the labs; test results became the literature of his life.

Resting against her leg, the phone rings.

Hugh's voice seems woody and resonate over the phone and she is certain that this is the first time she has *really listened* to his voice, although they had exchanged bits of talk at the preschool, gathering the boys, and of course the other night, in the bar's vestibule.

"That's all right. I mean, sure, I was just sitting here."

"Oh, I just thought. Well, I wondered if you might want to have a cup of coffee sometime, maybe dinner."

"I'd like that," she says, holding the phone against her ear with her shoulder, walking to the window, seeing the shroud of her face until she's close enough to see the lights and the water and the bridge.

"I wasn't sure if you'd be. Well, I mean I wasn't certain

if this was exactly the right time and everything."

He seems eager to get off the phone, but a date had to be set.

"I have a sitter. Jenny. So any night's fine," she says.

"All right then."

They settle on the next Wednesday, December 12, and she pauses long enough to make him think she is penciling it in because she says, "I'll pencil it in and call Jenny," and as soon as the phone is back in the cradle she picks it up again and calls Jenny.

"I have this tape," she tells Meg in the kitchen. They're sipping coffee, lifting the cups slowly. An old river house, the kitchen is on the bottom floor. A barge lulls up the river outside.

"Of me and Ron, on our honeymoon. Doing it."

Meg sips her coffee, draws a finger across one brow, and looks away from Grace out at the bare dirt of the garden and past that to the line of marl formed by the outgoing tide. The sun glimmers off the slick muck.

"He's not even cold yet," Meg says, lightly enough to make it a joke.

Grace imagines the steaming corpse up on the hill behind the hospital, buried with celebrities and nonentities alike. Steam rising up through the thick soil and the tree roots and the burlap winter turf. Meg looks at the tape, lifts it into her fingers. Her nails are long but she knows how to handle things with them.

"Can you, like, see much?"

"See much?"

"Yeah, I mean I tried that once with—what's his name?—

well, we could hardly make anything out, really."

"Well, we used an old camera, and the lighting sucked, but it's pretty clear what's going on."

"What are you going to do with it?"

"I don't know."

Meg stands, smooths down the sides of her skirt and looks out again at the view, and then goes into the play-room.

"Maybe you should toss it," she says, coming back with Billy, zipping his coat up to his chin. Billy looks at them betrayed, and says, "I don't wanna go. I don't wanna go. I don't wanna go."

"We've gotta go or we're not going to make it to Dr. Drake's," Meg says. She leans close to Grace and whispers, "He's got a series of booster shots to look forward to."

There will be a cocksure quality to Hugh's voice; he'll be wearing a brown tweed sports coat and an unfashionable wide tie of navy blue and red stripes; he'll have the leathery skin of a man who spends time outdoors; his knuckles have thick wrinkles that disappear when he makes a fist, and he has the kind of hands, fingers wide, flat-tipped, that can wield a pick with ease, clutch hunks of igneous rock, fist shale samples. Of course his interests will be varied and he'll say to her that he—like she—is very interested in music, and she'll say that she was a music major in college, even did some composing afterwards, a few pieces for piano, one for a small ensemble orchestra performed at a new music festival in Brooklyn before the kids came along and she gave it up, or rather sidetracked it, put it on the back burner. He'll mention his theory on

Glenn Gould's Bach, that the very secret to the universe lies between the discourse—the give and take between voices—on his Goldberg Variation, the first fast mono one, not the later one where he slowed stuff down and made even more noise—creak of his seat and his perpetual hem and haw along with himself, and that it has something to do with the way Gould pointed the notes, plucked them, and never used his sustain pedal. Hugh gets misty-eyed just talking about it. She'll gently mock him by mentioning how fashionable it has become to love Gould. He's hip, she'll say. There was that movie about his life. Drugs did him in. He did drugs in. Everything as fine as his playing gets twisted by fashion, turned into a prop, a commodity, a slot. Nodding and agreeing, he'll mention his love of Indian myths, Native American stories—whatever the hell you want to call the lore of dispossessed progenitors . . . After dinner they'll have a cognac at the bar downstairs before they pass out into the cold, newly fallen snow. First storm of the year. The roads shut down. The sidewalks empty. He'll walk her to the house—his own is up the hill, and he'll have to backtrack to get home, but he'll insist he doesn't mind. When they get to her house, Jenny, lying on the couch but not asleep, will sit up but not stand when she sees him. She occasionally babysits for Hugh's youngest boy—but suddenly he seems unfamiliar. She'll nod the way you'd nod to a passing stranger. ("He was coughing a bit. He's getting something," she'll say.) Down in the kitchen—getting her boots on—Jenny will ask, How was your date? In a soft, conspiratorial voice. His footsteps thud overhead as he moves around in front of the bookshelves, poking titles with one of his fingers. It was fine. All right. She'll try hard not to connect with Jenny's eyes, beset with a calm judgmental passivity. He'll be sitting in the big reading chair when she goes back up the stairs; he'll be fingering a copy of *Dubliners*, flicking the pages with his thumb as if he were speed reading the thing (or perhaps a book of Eliot poems; or Gary's battered *Winnie the Pooh*—anything really to indicate a secondary interest in books, to divide his attention); he's moving his eyes over her black turtleneck sweater, licking the smooth underside of her chin with his glance—and that's how she'll think of it, later, feeling his groping finger spider over her bra clasp; it's all right to lick someone with your eyes, to manifest your touch in different ways. What one might see as succumbing—swiftly undressing, actually helping him figure out the arrangement of the little hooks, laughing lightly at it, letting him enter her after only a few minutes of foreplay, his hands ungraceful and stupid in their windshield-wiper waves across her breasts. What one might see as a betrayal of Ron, might for her be nothing but a decisive fake to the universe. A grace. A giving to her pain. The tightness in her throat finally easing after two months. The gooseflesh along the inside of her arm, a cool tingle of nerves, fading with orgasm.

Meg, can you fuck your way out of grief? She'll say it suddenly in the kitchen, another day, weeks later. The same setup: having coffee in the kitchen while the kids play in the other room. Except it's February. Almost two months have passed. For the first time in years the river is frozen. Hunks of ice clog the sides, pounded up into piles. Last night, on her fourth date with Hugh, she went to a movie at the new multiplex; a late dinner at a bad Italian restaurant; then upstairs to her bedroom where he made love to her for the first time from above and behind, nothing but air and his sliding; the simplicity of the position, the way he loomed over her but didn't touch her except for the plunging, got her thinking about empty space. It was too easy. That position, her face in the pillow. How good it was. Meg pauses a moment, looks into her eyes, and then abruptly squeals and says her name—Grrraace Smith—elongating it like she's announcing a talk show host, and then stands and moves over to her, giving her a girlish hug, small, quick clasps. What's on your mind? Guiding Grace to the table and making her sit down. And right then she'll tell her about doing it with Hugh, confess how good it was from the start that very first night when she just went ahead and slept with him, and how she feels guilty about it but knows that there isn't anything wrong with getting pleasure out of her body. He has good hands, she'll say. He goes just the right speed. I'm so ashamed. I mean it hasn't been that long since Ron died and the truth is, I mean it's so horrible to say but I feel like, well, I feel I have to say it. He's better than Ron was, maybe, I mean maybe I'm fooling myself, maybe I don't remember or it doesn't matter—after all, he's gone physically, at least, and all that, and I shouldn't be comparing, right, shouldn't even put them side by side, but that's only natural, isn't it? And, yeah, well I have to admit that even when Ron was fine, before he got sick, you know, things weren't so great in that department even then, at least I didn't know they weren't great but now I do; I have to compare, can't help it, and I'd be dishonest if I didn't say that even though he's kind of awkward at times, he's a hundred times better than

Ron ever was because, well, because of something, his rhythm, I guess—he's very musical. He's fantastic, a virtuoso performance every time.

She imagines he'll take her farther away from the town on dates, their relationship burgeoning out in concentric circles, like the damage zones of a ground zero atomic blast. They'll go for rides with Gary on weekends, and Rudy and Stan, his boys, will come over and play, Stan perhaps acting the part of big brother. They'll drive up to West Point in the spring to watch the cadets parade. Then one night—almost a year later—early fall, they'll go over the Bear Mountain bridge alone and take the winding road north along the river. She'll kick off her pumps and wade her stocking toes through the hot wash of air from the heater—her hand resting plaintively on his knee, twitching along his wide-wale cords, zipping the fabric, brushing the knotty tightness of his crotch. A year has passed. The pain has faded. What she can recall of her life with Ron has become burnished, ideal, a beautiful relic (or the inverse; the whole marriage pure boredom, the man a dullard, the end inevitable one way or another). She'll look out the window at the wintry dark—barely listening to Hugh as he talks about a castle up on the hillside, built by a robber baron, and how he had once hiked up along a path to see the ruins of a house, the stone foundation loaded with charred timbers. They'll get to the town, park along the streets. A light snow will be falling. The restaurant at the end of the street, along a pier, will have long, wide windows allowing a view of the river—and across it—past the narrow bend of water—the tall looming dark

squat rock of Storm King Mountain; he'll explain something about how these rocks were not carved out by gla-
cial backwash. She only half listens. She has grown
accustomed to his voice, the resonate tones, and his soli-
loquies about geological formation; his world is striated
and broken and governed by forces webbing back into
some primordial center; he has a firm grip on this world,
on life, and he has lifted her up, has her in his arms, in the
parking lot, after the meal, and she smells a faint hint of
his spice cologne rising from damp wool. The engagement
ring is a bit loose on her finger. She keeps it bent slightly
during the ride home. Grief has lost a toehold. It has become only a faint residue.

When the thought occurred she was in the kitchen, mixing clots of chocolate powder into a glass of milk. *This
must not transpire. I can't let this happen.* Wednesday, December 12th. Out the window the river was flat, quivering
like molten silver. In the other room Gary and Billy were
playing. A potted fern sent FTD sat in the center of the
table next to a pile of papers she had to go through—
insurance reports, tax papers, bills, things that needed to
be sorted. She'd foist the fern on Meg; it was a late arrival,
a last-ditch effort at consolation. In a basket beneath the
table she put the card with the rest; there were hundreds—
people she'd never heard of from LA; movie people who
poured their condolences dishonestly the same way they
poured their praise thoughtlessly (if something you did
was connected to the production of cash). She sensed a
ruthless, grotesque quality in the arrival of this fern: it was
from Ron's old agent, a husky loud-mouthed cog in a mega-

agency who had been a part of Ron's life during those few intense years he was trying his hand at screenplays.

It did snow that night—Wednesday, December 12, 1999. And they did sit across from each other at the Hudson House and converse. His skin *was* weathered, and he talked about Iceland most of the time until rising naturally out of his talk was the suggestion that perhaps she might want to see the country someday; nothing about dancing on the lip of volcanoes, or throwing themselves into one sacrificially, but a hint of it. He had wide wrists and a habit of clasping his hands in a prayerlike manner. His voice had a languid, serene quality—maybe a bit too comfortable—as he talked over his divorce and the subsequent years of single-fatherhood (four years in all, but sounding like a lifetime).

"I can't say I'm a particularly lonely man," he said near the end. It was late. The waiters stood bored in the back of the restaurant. One was poking information into a computer window screen. From the windows came a brittle hiss of snow against glass. The air smelled of singed beef; of cigarette smoke drifting up from the bar downstairs.

"That's a funny way to put it. I mean the 'particularly.' You don't sound too sure."

"I know. I find myself, well, I guess it's the scientist in me. I can't help it. I look at my life objectively. I like to stand back. I think lonely people are the other way. They close in on themselves and never get the overall picture."

"I guess I'm one of those lonely people. I'm not much of a scientist. I flunked biology. All I remember is not being able to do that . . ."

"Do what?" he fingered his glass, held it high, looking through the fluted stem at her.

"Stand back from it all. I think it was a cat we did in biology."

"Ah, a cat. A dissection."

"Yes."

"Scientists are rarely lonely."

"Well," and then, before she could continue her response, the waiter came with the coffee and the conversation lulled in his presence and never returned to the subject. From that point on it was casual small talk, and then downstairs, in the street, the surprise of another fresh inch of snow; the walk home; paying Jenny, the short conversation with her in the mudroom—"How's it going?" "Fine, fine." "We had a good time." "Thank you for sitting." "Be safe, the sidewalks are slick." And then they were alone with the soft culling voice of Gary's breath through the monitor.

There are legends—the White River Sioux believe in Takuskanskan, the power of motion, a spirit behind all movement—and then there's our own bland myth of sexual intercourse, that somehow souls can become transfigured in the act; that all that motion, shifting, shoving, and grunting, can remake us.

Alone on Sunday morning in his colonial up the hill, Hugh sat at a wide, oval table, facing the window, cradling coffee in a big mug he'd bought in Germany during a rock conference; in the other room the boys were watching television—a soft dribble of sound effects, of high-pitched voices. His life had changed. Of that much he was sure. There was confusion, a slight, spongy befuddlement in the center of his head. In his chest—beneath his ribs—a vacuum had formed and he was certain that it was the first stages of a mild depression settling in. To combat it he'd take a pill and drive the boys to Bear Mountain and rent skates and do laps, work on his backwards crossover. The feel of the blades as he walked along the rubber matting, just before he stepped on the ice, would set him straight. Afterwards he'd take them to the lodge for hot chocolate and then, with the dull blue, pre-Christmas twilight settling in, he'd drive home, following the ribbon of red taillights down the Hudson Valley. He'd feel better alongside a thousand other souls—all draining themselves back into a Sunday evening. Maybe when he got back to the house he'd call Grace. Maybe not. It was doubtful. She was a strange case. Too much dead weight. This morning he didn't feel like the life-saving type. Anyway, there was a single woman named Ann he was thinking about. She worked at the reference desk at Columbia's Butler Library. In the course of research for his book, a geological history of Iceland, he'd flirted with her enough to know she'd probably accept his offer of dinner in the country—a ride up the Saw Mill; she could spend the night (he'd take the couch and send the boys to friends' houses), or he'd even drive her back in.

But his life had changed. It would never be exactly the same. The strangeness of that night would be hard to shake.

She had it set up, the VCR tape already inside. (When she inserted it, she felt the longing desire of the machine for the tape. It was the smaller camera cassette nestled within a larger shell mechanism that yawned the tape outward against the kiss of the playback head, all clamps and rollers and pins stretching taut.) She pushed play. Beside her on the couch, Hugh watched with a placid gaze—an expectant and politely curious look on his face as he crossed his legs and put his heel softly on top of the coffee table. His shoes were off. There were gold toes on the end of his socks and the copy of *Dubliners*, bound in dark green, on his lap. She hadn't said much, just a murmur about wanting to watch something, and that was it, and the truth was, and she'd think about this later, he didn't ask what she was going to show him. He didn't care to find out ahead of time what in particular she was going to put on the screen. There wasn't *a need in him to know*. It didn't matter. What she'd decided to put in front of him by the way of entertainment was beside the point; the point was elsewhere. So the machine did the little windup sound— all that tension; there was a blip, a blue screen, then a black screen with some white sinews of static along the bottom—and then, appearing out of the darkness, fading long and opening like a cornucopia of light and body parts, the scene of her and Ron making love on their honeymoon; first a blur, then dissolving (as she imagined Hugh saw it) through the darkness, a puzzle of light, the crack of Ron's ass and her legs parted wide, in and out of focus at the same time, all accompanied by the sound of their soft moans and the camera motor—the hiss of the air conditioner, and behind that, the motorbikes buzzing down the *avenida*.

"What's this?" Hugh said, with a slight start, landing flat on each word.

"It's me and Ron," she answered; she was on the floor

with her legs tucked beneath her, to the side, sitting half-way between the TV set and the couch.

"Exactly," he said.

He might have said Shut it off, out of some kind of disgust, or shame; or he might have been turned on by the sad ordeal of watching her dead husband doing it to her; she might have stood up tearfully and shouted Look at what the world took from me, but instead there was the soft clatter of the storm windows catching a hard burst of wind from the north; there was the background hum of the camera motor's resonating off the Spanish dressing table; the soft clutch of two people reaching an early orgasm against their wills; her legs clamping tight around the back of his thighs; nothing funny at all this time; it seemed a vastly different tape than the one she'd viewed with Ron on the small television in their apartment in the city. (The current television was twice as big.) Hugh sat back watching and didn't say anything. He did so partly out of a politeness for her feelings; to stand and walk away—considering the sanctity of the situation—wouldn't be kind; he had to at least see a conclusion to the night, so he watched for four minutes until the awkward disengagement after the orgasm, the parting of flesh from flesh, and saw the pixels of light add up to what seemed to be a template for the home-brewed porn tape. (He'd never rented one of those amateur porn tapes from the video store before, but this was exactly what he'd expected.) He watched the end and sat still while she shut it off, drew both hands through her hair, and told him he'd better go as she led him down the stairs to the mudroom door where he left his boots, and thanked him for the wonderful night while he tied his laces. Then, as she held his coat for him, he urged his arms through the sleeves; and she spoke the whole time about the breaded pork she'd had for dinner, and how nice the Hudson House atmosphere was, until he turned and said, "Hang in there," and gave her a little hug, making out through his down coat the softness of her shoulders. He then trudged his way up the hill to the main street, turned left, and walked through town. His hood was up and the asthmatic seethe of his breath kept him company. He was a scientist, used to looking at facts, but he wasn't hard-hearted. He knew what was up. The game was clear. She wanted to nix it, to throw it at him, her life before Ron's death. She wasn't ready to love again. It was too early. Her heart was still with Ron, as it should be. She was perfectly normal. Nothing was wrong with what she did, showing him the tape like that, acting out a commendable faithfulness to her past; it was the kind of impulsive, perhaps deranged action you'd expect from a widow. Strangely, he thought, it was (he was now hiking up the hill in jerky, quick strides) what you want from a widow. You want that soft sadness. You want the strange behavior—wild, passionate moodiness. You want pain manifested in deviant acts. There was a fine snow falling, melting as it hit his face. Grief seemed to crunch beneath his feet. The whole planet was a matrix of movements, he knew, causing irremediable change. He thought of Iceland, of the wild surges of gradient heat buried beneath the sea—of the long fissures of magma basting into the immense pressure of the depths, just twelve feet of water equaling the pressure of miles of air, and deeper still into a fantastic weight. In a week, back in Iceland for the conference on plate tectonics, he'd relax and think things over. He'd think only about geothermal system problems, precise yet still earthly and ultimately ungraspable. He'd take the boat out to the site of their study and dive with his colleagues. He'd gone down before in the Alvin—the only thing between his life and those tremendous pressures, a rubber gasket on the door. Pure titanium walls, five thick feet of it, but all that came between life and death was that gasket. He loved Iceland. There was no end to the amount of warmth they could tap from the earth—absolutely free. It was never cold inside a home in Iceland. The price: fantastic volcanic instability, the insecurity of knowing that at any moment, any day, the whole place might go up in a blast. He was at his door. His hand was on the knob. He had so much to do. He had to think it all over and come to some conclusion.

The boys were asleep. Upstairs he undressed in the dark and left his clothes on the floor. He didn't brush his teeth. The cognac buzz was wearing off, and there was an aftertaste of dinner in his mouth. He lay and watched the dark shadow branches on the ceiling. There was a steady, hard wind. He kept his eyes open for as long as he could. When he closed them, he saw floating behind his eyelids the shadows from the videotape, half formed, Grace's knees and the back of Ron's thighs, blended through the light and the lens of that afternoon in Madrid; although he couldn't precisely identify the sound, he could hear the buzz of the motorbikes winding through the narrow, ancient streets.

TAHORAH

HE WAS in the CCU and sick of all the barbaric grunts and cries coming from next door and out in the hallway. What name to pin them with he wasn't sure, something foreign because the lingo they were speaking made no sense and got on his nerves almost as much as the crying and sobbing and all that, but he couldn't do anything about it because he was soaking in morphine and wasn't concerned about *the details;* he gave up on the details after the second heart attack, all that pain, big walls of it, like in the movies, groaning and trying to guide the truck over to the side; where was this? A hundred and fifty miles outside of Altoona? Almost home? Somewhere in Jersey? No one on the medical staff seemed to know, or care. The crunch of gravel on the breakdown lane, the smooth, low scrape as he hit the guardrail, the scream of plastic bumper stuff peeling off—and then skidding like that, rolling partway over, up on the side, his cab, deep crimson red, while the trailer ripped loose and flipped and tumbled down the hill. The babble of prayer—that's what was coming from next door, he knew, at least some little part of him knew. Some of them were jawing away at it right outside his door. And here's the guy Angela sent saying *Our prayers are with you* and talking, his lips close to his ear, Listerine breath, one of those huge brows—a real caveman, this preacher from the Bethel First Christ down in Rutherford, or near there. It's Angela's idea of a bad joke, a last hurrah, knowing damn well he wouldn't want it, probably making up a long story about her ex-husband and guilt and how she felt he needed consolation and affirmation in what were surely to be his final hours. Now along with the carrying on in the hall there was the mumbling pious tones of this guy's voice to contend with, too, talking something about the narrow way of Christ; funny that it was the only thing he knew, or felt like knowing, about his heart, the narrow closing of that artery clogged with too many donuts and too much coffee and long hours on the road popping crank, mixing vodka with whatever the hell he got his hands on the last few years doing transcon runs of whatever freight he could land. Hitch your cab to the trailer and ask no questions.

When they tried to get the shunt in, the artery collapsed on itself, final and for good, and he had a second coronary right on the table. Nothing to do now, the doctor said, except wait out the twenty-four-hour grace or lack of grace period, the rough time, and hope for the best, because no matter what, part of his heart was permanent dead matter. "If you're gonna die," the doc said, "it's most likely gonna be in the next twenty-four hours."

Now this dwarf priest or whatever lecturing him on Christ's narrow way.

"What do you want, Father?" His lips would barely open, corrugated with dryness. His mouth had been dry all night, dry into the day, and was now dry in the afternoon no matter how many of the little plastic cups of cranberry juice he sucked down.

"Father?" the guy said, softly. Then he cleared his throat. "You don't have to address me that way."

"What are you doing here, Father?"

"I'd prefer Bill, if you don't mind."

"All right, Bill," he said, his lips contorted around the words the way they do in a movie when the soundtrack is off slightly.

The preacher, or minister, or pastor seemed uncomfortable standing and went to get a chair, pulling it over with a loud screech, sitting up close to the bed, then leaning his arms on the rail and looking down at his charge.

"I've come to deliver unto you the word of God," the guy said, speaking in what was mostly a mumble, hardly audible over the beeps and sighs of the machines; tubes and wires yanked on his chest and arms and legs. Just then, before the preacher could begin yapping again, there was a sudden, persistent beep. A nurse came in quickly and pulled the white cotton blanket down from his neck and exposed the deep, dark curls of chest hair and prodded it until that sustained beep stopped and only his heart rate was left, and the smooth gulps of the balloon machine, the aortic counter-pulsation device. Minister Bill moved his chair back and sat quietly during all this. All for the better. He was wading through the softness of the morphine, or whatever pain reliever he was on. The word of God could wait. But then the nurse left and the preacher pulled his chair back, picking it up this time, and leaned on the rail again and began talking about the *way* of God and Christ, the whole rigmarole, talking about how much Angela loved him even though the scag hadn't been in touch since '76, good old bicentennial: twenty years, he thought, and then it came to a dwarf priest blabbing about his favorite hymn, something like "O Worship the King, All Glorious Above," and quoting it to him, his medicinal breath up close, taking advantage of his helplessness to get right in there, not even a half foot from his face, and even singing it a little bit—a kind of singsong lullaby, "frail children of dust, and feeble as frail, in thee do we trust, nor find thee to fail," and then he said to the dwarf priest, having to really dig to talk, "Father, do me a favor. Shut up. Or speak in tongues if you want. But if you sing any more, I'll get out of this frickin' bed and break your neck."

It was down in Tennessee—on a run to Florida with a load of machine parts—that he saw the speaking-in-tongues church. Hooked up with a girl named Lauren, sweet girl, at a truck bar, ended up in her trailer screwing away and then the next day, Sunday, being dragged to her church and watching them blabbing in their snakelike tongues. He left the church, got his rig warmed up, and headed south, pronto. Now in the room, with Father Bill there in the chair sitting silently, he hears that sizzle of voices out in the hall, a whole family grieving over some loss, hacking away in their language, then bits of English, then their language again. Other times blending the two; all melded together into a hiss that seemed like the ones used by those speaking in tongues that morning down in whatever podunk state he happened to be in—Tennessee or Kentucky.

For a second he wants to ask this preacher about Angela, just how she's doing, but he knows the guy, most likely sworn not to disclose anything, will just say *Fine, fine,* and leave it at that. What else was he going to say? That she was wallowing in shit, dirt poor, missing payments on that piece-of-crap house on Elmwood, or Shorthills? For all he knew she wasn't there anymore, but he thought of it anyhow when he thought of her, with the kids, toiling away over a tub of dirty clothing and a washboard or something—nothing real. When he imagined it, that's how it was, images out of someplace that never existed because he couldn't remember what had existed. The house they owned in Rutherford. A simple clapboard number, a Sears catalog house. A nice weedy yard with one of those clothes-drying trees, and always laundry on it like a blooming white rose of sheets and underwear when he got home from work the one year he was working steady, providing, doing his bit; old preacher Bill wouldn't admit, if asked, that she was bathing in pain like he was, maybe worse off, cancer of the brain, an invalid, or nuts, bedded full-time in some ward someplace. Of course she was fine, Bill would say. He tried to remember what she looked like and got a vision of her dark red hair, wide oval face, smooth, very white skin, and her lively laugh. He got a vision of her at the cabin they rented upstate, down by the water, toking on hand-rolled smokes and drinking beer until they ended up in the bed, a rattling iron thing, with their clothing off and only that pale summer twilight, half there, half gone, making their skin smooth as whole milk; such wonderful smoothness, he recalled, especially at the flat of her belly going down, down to the pubis bone, the hard ridge on both sides, and with the breeze like that, not too hot or too cool coming through the screens.

When he woke it was night, pale green light from the screen overhead and hard orange parking-ramp lights in the window. From the hallway came a pure, downy, neon brilliance. Father Bill had vanished, his chair empty where he left it near the door. The light throb of the pump going; the faint pulse of the device in his chest cavity opening up with air and deflating next to his heart like a little bird nesting between his ribs.

How long he lay he didn't know; hours, minutes. Just the machine and a few cries in the hall—Arabic or something, some little kid making wailing noises, the family still gathered out there but kind of quiet and silent now, maybe it was too late, asleep the lot of them out in the lounge with the others. There had to be plenty; a big hospital, overcrowded, lots of dying going on in the ICU and the CCU.

One of the docs came in looking over the charts and poking around and not talking much because he knew better, knew this old codger who'd been dragged in off the highway had a nasty temperament and didn't care much for small talk. A few pokes and probes, a check of the data on the screen.

"We're going to remove the balloon pump," he said.

"We've gone long enough now and it's a pretty pricey hunk of machinery, and there's a patient just coming out of emergency surgery who's going to need it right off. The police might drive another one over from Newark, but I think you're stabilized enough now."

Strapped beneath his leg was a long plank to keep things flat and even, and in his leg, up near his crotch, was a hole about the size of a dime but feeling more like a quarter to him, a hole leading into the femoral artery. A hole in his frickin' leg, he'd thought a few dozen times, and not a bullet hole. He'd thought that if he ever had a real hole in his leg—a genuine hole—it would've been from a bullet from one of the skags at the crappy bars he frequented en route from CA to NY. The nurses came in—a Hispanic girl, a bit on the plump side, but he'd take her anyhow if he had the heart—hardy har, har—and a large older woman with blue-gray hair, and then a male nurse; all three held on to him, gripping different parts of him while the doc slowly drew the balloon out from against his heart, pulling the wire through the dime-sized hole, drawing it down his femoral artery where it shouldn't have been and sure as fuck couldn't fit because the pain was red-hot, explosive, convulsive, and he screwed up his face—all jawbone and sun-weathered crags—and screamed like a stuck pig: "Give me some fricking painkillers, you morons, you mooorrrrons," while the doc jammed something that looked like a wine bottle opener over the hole and gave one last little tug and got it out, not a word, working silently except for a little murmur of directions to one of the nurses.

"Sorry." The doc shrugged.

"I'll bet you are." He could barely speak. The pain was making bursts of sparks on the inside of his eyelids.

The nurses and doc exchanged glances, as if to say: *This one's a real nasty bastard, keep your distance; if we could we'd put a muzzle on him, costing the hospital money and the government money and the whole world bits of spirit;* but the doc put his hand on the guy's forehead and rubbed it there a little bit. He kept his hand there way too long to be any kind of test for fever or a thump to listen to something.

"What happened to preacher man?" he said.

"Excuse me," Doc said.

"The pastor, the Bible-thumper, what happened to him?"

"Can't help you there."

Then they left him alone with the hard throb of the pain, or the remains of the pain, because that's how it was, like a swish of chalk on a board or an imprint or something—a feeling all the way up his leg and into his empty chest, now without the little nesting bird, nothing but frickin' air and his own heart bobbing away in there—a feeling of the pain of that thing being yanked down the inside of his leg by the moron doctor. A soft, faint beep from the machine indicating his pulse and him alone and the noise in the hall kind of getting louder with the babble and all that, more voices, the soft squeak of tennis sneakers on the waxed floor; another set of steps, more, and more.

In the hall, before he came out and placed his ghostly visage before them, hanging with tubes and in his flimsy gown, gasping for air, the family was bunched up to the side, praying, talking, crying—two little kids allowed on the unit only because it was the last few hours, if not minutes, of Tara's life. A few days ago the doctors put her chances at slim to none—or they laid it out in some numbers, most likely, trying to keep it mathematical, the odds, because whenever you were talking about lost youth—death at an early age—you had to couch things as much as you could in figures. Tara's father was wearing, and had been for two days, a dark brown tweed sports coat, penny loafers, a pair of Docker khakis, and had his head buried in his hands. He was slouched down against the wall, talking to himself, jouncing his heels against the floor. Next to him, seated on the floor listening, was Stanley, his brother, who, upon getting the news, had flown in directly from Israel; he was jet lagged and exhausted and felt himself floating in a bedazzling clean space of the hallway; he'd been there all afternoon, trying to soothe the soul of his poor brother, from whom he'd been estranged. All because of what? A bad shipment of goods he'd sent over, or lined up; nothing really his fault at all—he'd been nothing but the usual middleman, but the deal somehow wedged in between the men and, after a while, except for enough small pleasantries meant to keep at least an outward semblance of civility (mainly, it had to be admitted, for the women), the two rarely spoke; the bad deal became large over time—the sum of money lost debated—until everything else that had happened before that, all the way back to petty squabbles over marble games on the dirt tarmac outside their apartment in Israel, each tense moment, seemed prophetic. Flying out, for Stanley, who was fearful of elevators and tall buildings, had been a grand gesture, a great flourishing of his arms outward over the skies of Tel Aviv (as he saw it); a token of his true, deep love, a love that went beyond that bad deal (five thousand pipe wrenches; all of them forged with a wobbling claw); but of course what did one expect from a deeply grieving brother except this—this wagging of the body to the song of sorrow? This sniffing and depleted man at a loss as to what might, what can, what should be done? So all Stanley did was sit with his brother, listen, nod, murmur agreements, add a few comments now and then in Hebrew (presuming—perhaps wrongly—that it would help Howard just to hear the mother tongue). Behind them, in the room with Tara, the women were around the bed, resting the tips of their fingers on the bedding, brushing the hair back from her forehead. A car had gone through a stop sign in Hackensack—a Saturday afternoon, light traffic for that corner, an elderly man driving a pale green Buick Skylark with his blood level four times above the legal limit sped right through and broadsided her Toyota at seventy-five miles an hour.

When she got close to the end—and they could tell, or rather the nurses indicated it silently by nods of the head and slight eye movements—there was a quieting. Calls went out from the pay phone in the lounge, where people limp in their anxiety lay sprawled over huge, square-cut maroon chairs. To speak the words that he had to speak— not that she was dead but that she was, as they said (although he thought it was kind of a phony phrase) near death (as if death were an island, a vacation resort), Stanley found himself listening to his own voice: he was a dummy; some other guy was holding him, composed and serene and bearing terrible news, the ventriloquist, as he spoke he heard his own voice quiver—dry and husky from the long flight—beneath the weight of the news he had to offer up; at the same time, he was thinking of the old radio show routines he and Howard had loved so much as a kid.

With the pump removed from his chest, everything out in the hall became amplified by the silence. He didn't know it, but the prayers were in Hebrew, mainly, although some were in English, and some of what he heard was just talking, and crying, and emotive phrases such as *how can it be?* and *why why why* and *if only* and *oh God.* And a rocking motion verbalized in a kind of cantorial singsong— and even a little actual singing from one of the really little kids who didn't know what was going on, a rapturous little tune with senseless lyrics about a goat and a shoe and the Fourth of July.

Just before he dragged himself up, decided to shut them up out there, he remembered there had been a night right after that night upstate, with the wonderful breeze through the screen, when he and Angela had sat on the end of the dock drinking beers and watching the stars clarify and listening to the fish rise, splashing, mostly bluegills but some pretty good largemouth bass he was sure. (He'd spent that afternoon casting a huge spoon, loaded up with worms, to no avail.) Up and down the shore the fish were leaping like mad while behind Angela, in the thick darkness under the trees, firefly light was being exchanged in frantic waves up and down the beach.

"What'cha thinking?" he asked her.

"I'm just thinking, you know, about all we're gonna do and how good it's gonna be and all that," she said. It was a song she was singing, her own little hymn to the portents the future held.

"Hummm," he said, taking a huge slug on his beer, a sizzle down his throat.

"And what'cha thinkin' yourself?"

"About nothing, nothing at all except being here and how good it is here, with you, now." And he meant it. His middle brother Gary had died a year before working a roofing job, and shaking the grief of that loss, the recurrent image of the idiot slipping on a loose slate and falling two stories, breaking his neck, had until that very moment seemed impossible; now something was lifting, or at least that's what he felt, recalling that night on the dock with Angela while he, in turn, lay flat on his back in the hospital with his blood pumped full of morphine; the same bright lifting, like he was flying up over the lake. Some kind of grace, a moment of it, on the end of the dock with the shore webbed in the light of fireflies.

One might hope for some kind of divine justice. An amazing feat how he got himself up and dragged himself into the hall to scream at them, considering the odds, the wires and tubes and warning beeps, the very low flow pressure his heart offered. He spoke his mind out there in the hall, shouting at them. If God had been just, he would've slammed him with an occlusion; a major, major infarct that locked his heart into a knot, a clench of fibers so tight, a fist in the center of his rib cage, a burst of blinding pain that sent him stumbling, gasping for his last. Instead he had a minor event—one he hardly felt at the time.

He did die. He died a few days later, alone, in the mid-

dle of the night, when a series of infarctions began and he
went into a major arrest and the staff came in and performed heroic measures (because he said hell no to that
living will crap. No way. Now how am I gonna sign that?
You'll put me under, for Christ's sake. Why should I trust
you morons after the way you jerked that fucking balloon
out of my leg?), giving him a zap with the jelled electrodes,
pumping him full of anticoagulants, working a sweat up
over the guy.

Seven days of mourning without the hard leather of shoes,
and during Shiva only once was the crazy guy mentioned;
brought up by Stanley—who in his grief had gone downstairs twice, out onto the sidewalk along Riverside Drive
to take in the fresh air off the Hudson and to sip single
malt from one of those little bottles he'd bought on the
flight over; he was on his third bottle. He was back inside
the apartment, on the floor, talking softly with Saul, a
buyer for the hardware chain, and in passing other sub-
jects, sliding through them in his buzz, he sadly mentioned
the Gentile who'd stumbled out into the hallway half
alive, filling the air with his foul curses; it was the way he
leaned into Saul; it was the way he tried to flatten his voice
out from his Hebraic to an Ohio twang (and trying to
whisper at the same time, too)—*Shut the fuck up for Christ
sake you babbling idiots; go back to where you came from.*
It was the form, not the content, that got the men laughing, just as Tara's father came down the stairs, arm in arm
with his wife.

Out the tall windows the Hudson glinted flecks of
white light, and spread before them was a view embracing

New Jersey across the river all the way up to the George Washington Bridge. When Tara died, the word went out via optical fibers, calls made to Israel, making sure everybody who had to mourn knew of her death so that no one would be called upon to begin mourning later, because from the moment the news was heard, those so obligated had to observe the laws and customs as set down in the Talmud. The ritual washing of the body, Tahorah, had been performed because none of her injuries, all internal and concussive, had drawn enough blood to soak her clothes, in which case she would have been buried in the bloodied garments. After the funeral they went to the cemetery, pausing the seven times to recite Psalm 91,

He that dwelleth in the secret place of the Most High
Shall abide under the shadow of the Almighty.

before spreading the dirt over the coffin.

While Stanley recounted the story of the crazy man in the hospital, upstairs in the bedroom her father had been ripping up all of his ties, one by one, and piling them aside. He rent each one apart, yanking hard and wide, skinny narrow ones from back in the early eighties, wide ones from the sixties with huge stripes, and semi-wide ones from the nineties. He tore them down the middle, if he could, and he tore them apart from the center, opening them up, plying apart the silk backing and ripping down the sides. His hands were dry and cracked and caught the silk. When his wife went up to see where he was, he was nearly finished, seated on the side of the bed next to a jostled pile of twisted fabric spilling over the edge of the poplin bedspread, doing one last tie, a Calvin Klein with deep blue triangles set in a lighter blue background beset with swirls and splats à la Jackson Pollock that Tara had given him for the holidays two years ago. Pollock had been her favorite artist. Maybe once every couple of weeks, for a year, he wore it, and then put it aside in favor of ones he had picked out himself, more conservative patterns. He had performed the standard Qeri'ah at the funeral, rending the tiny strip of ribbon pinned to his left lapel, but apparently that act hadn't been enough. Stop, his wife said. Stop. Stop. Stop. And he did, bowing his head into his palms and heaving out a long cry, kicking his heels into the carpet, cradling what was left of the tie up to his lips.

"Come downstairs with me," she said, placing her hand along the curve of his neck.

"All right. For you, I'll go downstairs," he cleared his throat and got up and slowly lifted a few strands of neckties onto the bed.

The faces seemed to have answers for him as he walked down the spiral stairs into the Shiva; people hunched down talking softly, moving food up to their mouths; he would remember seeing each face in turn: the tight lips of Erma, his wife's best friend, holding a sob; his business associates looking away, casting glances out over New Jersey; the kids obliviously playing with dolls near the entrance to the kitchen. But what he would remember the most, what he centered on later, was the strange, twisted smile on his brother's face, a blessed smile that seemed to go way back to their childhood secrets; it was the way Stanley smiled when he was trying not to smile, the tightness in the corners of his mouth that led to two half-moon dimples; a wonderful grimace and smirk combined; and seeing it, something lifted slightly. It was only the first bit of weight off of his grief but it was significant in that it was the first; he went over and the two men held each other, tighter and tighter.

"What are you laughing about?"

"Nothing."

"Come on."

"The foolishness of the world," Stanley said.

Out the windows the afternoon was waning. Beams of orange cut back between buildings in Jersey. The elongated shadows of buildings pressed behind the view.

It was never spoken of again, that scene, that moment in the hospital corridor. It didn't go down in family lore. It didn't go anywhere except for that moment into the smile on Stanley's face, the thing Tara's father saw when he entered back into the Shiva.

THE
GESTURE HUNTER

I'M INTERESTED in how people go about their daily lives. You know, how they bide their time, what they fill all that time up with. Not the big motions but the little ones, I suppose: someone hanging clothes on an old-fashioned line, breaking with the convention of the gas dryer, the fluid motion of her arms lifting the sheets, a wooden pin between her teeth, the sway of the line, laden with wind-blown sheets, in relation to how she bends up to it in greeting; a guy at the gas station helping the full-service customers, his foot on the black slab of rubber bumper, leg jittering hard as he pumps, the car rising and falling gently while his oblivious eyes stay cocked to some lost point on the horizon and he plucks at the stains under the arms of his green sweatshirt. I'm a gesture hunter. I seize moments. I care fully about them.

It was one of those days typical to our town, which is along the Hudson, just twenty-odd miles up from the city. I mean that the day had settled into the town and the town into the day—clear and sunny with just an edge of cool to the wind, which ruffled the surface of the river white and was strong enough to cause a few waves to curl up but not really break. (Most of the waves on the Hudson have a certain pathetic quality: weak-lipped, shaky. So do the boats, working the strange wind patterns, mainly from the north, trying to buck the tidal currents, coming about and then landing in irons in mysteriously dead winds beneath the Tappan Zee Bridge; nothing fluid or graceful about any of it.) It's odd that I can't tell exactly if it's the day coming into the town or the town coming into the day when I start out on these searches, especially in the morning—I start early sometimes—when the light is still low and silvery. But as I said, this was, it seemed, nothing but a typical day on all accounts, except that it was morning and I had started out rather early. I can't say now that I felt at that moment—as I made my first slow sweep through the center of town, taking Broadway (doesn't every town near the city have its own futile Broadway?), driving my usual five miles an hour—that I felt any sense of betrayal; I mean that I did not think the day had anything betraying in it destined for me. But days do that. A day can betray you. You invest in it and it gives something back you didn't expect. I saw from the corner of my eyes a man leaving the police station; he had a slow, elderly walk—very much like mine—a pale yellow shirt, and one of those crushable canvas hats you might use for fishing;

he was moving with his slow gait down the wheelchair ramp. Along the other side of the street, in front of one of the many antique shops (those scandalous resellers and repackagers of the past) that have given our town a place on the map, someone, lifting something, was halfway through the door. I saw just the back end of the man: his Wrangler jeans, his hip, and the edge of whatever he was carrying, dark oak maybe, and the buffed metal frame of the door. Nothing worth noting. A gesture, certainly, but not the kind I wanted. I needed the whole thing, united and graceful and, most of all, full of revelation, stark wonderful revelation; a young man carrying a table into a shop didn't cut it. Ahead, the light was green; farther ahead, maybe a block or two, one of those big, bulky, stupid emerald four-wheel beasts that roam our streets.

Let me here just make some notes, add some things: you see this is near the end of the century and certain movements of small towns as I used to know them, as I knew them growing up, are waning. When I was a boy in Galva, Illinois, there were wakening gestures to a town. All towns had them. They were infused with grace. Mr. Bursell of the dry goods store would waken in his little apartment over his store—moving with the deliberate, uncaring slowness of a permanent bachelor, lifting the spilled flower of his blue dungarees around his waist, looping the belt slowly as he looked out his window, across the street where Ellen Barton was sweeping the sidewalk in front of her husband's movie theater, The State. Ah, that gesture, the broom wedded to her arm and her arm to the broom and the swish motion, elbow bent, and the bits of ticket stub and tissue and popcorn being forced forward into the gutter. Her cool, honey hair up in a clip. The bleached pleats of her skirt around her ankles. Bursell would study that movement for a moment, fingers on his belt, and then make his way downstairs, going out the front, so he could crank the awning open over his store to hold the morning sunlight (later in the afternoon he'd do the same in reverse), taking the worn wooden spool that steadied the bar with one hand while with the other he had to crank. His cranking would lead the awning, tart green and white stripes, to open gracefully—his work taking shape and form over his head. That's how it used to be in a town that wasn't betrayed yet by the onslaught that would eventually take so many of the finer gestures out of our hands; stolen from us, taken into the innards of so many machines.

We are the graceless and dumbfounded, insane with our own insatiable desire for another time and place and a sense of movement, we gesture hunters. One movement of a tongue over a dry lip will do for us; a woman in the graveyard weeping at the foot of her husband's grave, her navy blue skirt hiked up over her calves, and the flat worn soles of her shoes the color of dry sand—that's just it, all we need, all we strive for in this world, nothing more or less. We have our modus operandi, our techniques, some preferring to await the passing of some perfect movement, to sit all day, day upon day, waiting. It's a heartless means of searching, I think, to let the movement of the town go about you, but there are those, my fellows, who are content to work that way; and I say, go your way in peace. In town there are two such operators, though their intentions I have to doubt somewhat; their desires are not so pure as mine. With his hair gone and blotches of Vietnam—napalm, some say—purpling his scalp, Hank sits patiently, welded to a bench, but his searches are invalidated by his heaving sucks from a tall-boy, the paper sack tight around the top of the bag and wet from condensation. And there is an old hag nicknamed Boop—à la Betty—who smells of urine and wears stained nylon stockings and tattered dresses but doesn't bring even the slightest glance from passersby as she maintains her place on the bench in front of the ice-cream shop, making her sputtering, inane sounds, clucks and quacks and hisses and an occasional word or two, maybe searching or maybe not. It's hard to know what to think of her, and I seldom do think of her if I can help it, but I do know that maybe at one time she was a gesture hunter, too, and went about it firmly and with all the good intentions one might expect. Long ago, when time was different and we were going about our business in town, she was the big realtor (and I, at the bank, the largest lender of funds). Then, as now, it was the duty of a realtor to bend and flex her personality to match those of a potential buyer, even going so far as to match him gesture for gesture when necessary: she might be standing in an inelegant little Cape Cod, with a bad roof of sagging rafters and a main beam ridden with termites, and still she'd have to throw her arms wide in one of those open embraces and take a deep chest-heaving breath of air as if it were the freshest in the world to match the gesture of the buyer, who, coming up from the city for a summer day of looking around, had happened into her office just to see what was available and, after seeing the Cape Cod, felt suddenly stunned by the idea of living in "the country." So with Boop it was hard to know; she'd stolen so many gestures, hugged them to her, that maybe she was looking for one of her own that had become lost out there. That's the basic nature of any of us hunters. We want above all to find what is rightfully ours.

Twice I've been consecrated by pure gestures—just twice if you discount the third incident. Once I took my late and long-lost son, Stevie, fishing up in Massachusetts; the Chesterfield River, rocky and hard-wading, day gone, faded, that blistering darkness pulling down midsummer slow over the water. We were holding out for the risers that were destined to come because there were spinners overhead, lowering themselves with the darkness like flecks of snow refusing to meet the earth. They were doing their copulation rite midair, and soon they would hit the water to lay their eggs. (I have not fished since that day, nor will I fish again.) Airfucks, we called them, one of those embarrassed dirty jokes between father and son that has a bitter taste now that he is gone and what was filthy between us is as dark as soot to my memory. It's all memory, and perhaps that's what makes the pain I caused him at that moment—just a sharp little barb in his wrist—stand out so acutely, and makes the gesture that followed his pain remain the cleansed and holy one (of the two), purified by time and memory and dust and all of that. He was working this deep oily pool that caught the night long before it fell, along a shale ledge, lounging his back against a large rock, casting and recasting while I worked my own pool along the other side. My backcast was caught by a single uprising of night breeze, the only one that night, as far as I recall, and to compensate I had to work my line sidelong, and then there was the sharp, startled sound of his voice cracking, returning to his child-voice, as I hooked him in the smooth white flesh of his wrist, not knowing I'd done so and thinking I was snagged, yanking thoughtlessly, just once, just once, but the pain I caused him is eternal and everlasting because and only because of his voice at that moment, mingled and mixed with the rabble of water over stone. You see, all this led up to the gesture pure and sweet, of his face, a large face, so much my face, smiling at the pain and flicking my fly back, swiping the blood from his wrist. Blood I couldn't see and will never see. It was the flick and the smile, barely visible, maybe not visible at all to me in the falling darkness, shadow-laden, deep and brooding, the woods pressing in, the sides of the gorge seeming to swell up into the woods. I had caused him sudden and inexplicable pain, and he had flicked it off, a simple gesture that continued in one fluid motion to his cast and his line being laid out over that dark pool. Later, the trout rose to take his fly and spun him into that wonderful motion of working a fish, force against force—not a pure gesture (there were only two) but worth saving nonetheless. When I learned that my son had been killed in Vietnam, taken by pains that must have flowered and exploded from back to front, blood pluming out his chest where the bullet left, I imagined that flick of the wrist, and I smiled and vowed to worship it and perhaps one day equal it. I vowed to find just once more a motion as graceful, just once more, on the surface of this earth peopled by human souls going about their lives, to find a gesture that equaled that of my son in the stream a year and a half before he died, or that of his sweet little wet body in a tub, the scent of baby soap . . .

That day, now, returning to that day with the morning sky opening up and the white haze down near the edge of the river, having passed that man going into the antique store, the stoplight changing to amber, then red, with that strange slowness only I seem to notice. The police were on to me. They knew about my search and often pulled me over. There was nothing illicit in my circling route, down Broadway five or six blocks and then back around, close to the river, where the new housing developments hunched and cluttered. On some days I'd settle myself into the bench in front of the library to examine movements and gestures in a small quadrant: I'd see good things there occasionally, the passing motions and gestures of many, but rarely anything close to a pure gesture. Only once, almost, catching sight of two folks bedecked in khaki pants and matching navy polo shirts, working their way across the street with that retired stride you see up here, proud and purposeful lopes of the legs slightly bent and distorted by hidden pains and aberrations, bones brittle and weakening; these two were spry on their feet, and their gesture held me for weeks, sustained me in my search, filled my soul with bubbles of possibilities. She held him as they crossed, a light little clutch, her fine fingers curled around one of his, which one not mattering the least to me, because in a good gesture it is the gesture itself that demolishes and makes irrelevant the smaller details; the whole thing becomes a movement, a blemish, an act unto itself apart from the particulars. In the hopes of more, I thought about follow-

ing them, but then I knew better. To hunt gestures you
have to let them find you, blowing across the street like
dead leaves: a man lingers over something in the window,
his hands in his pockets in a particular way; a young child
waves silently with a subdued manner to nothing at all as
she passes in the back seat of a blue Chevy Nova, her eyes
dogged and lonely.

That morning when the traffic light changed I made
my way forward through the intersection, looking from
one side to another, as is my habit. Just past the corner of
Broadway and Elm, I felt that strange sensation one gets
looking from a main street down a side street, a street leading down to the river, the haze of light as it bleeds from
the water, the close proximity of the dusty brick walls, the
loneliness that such side streets sing. Long ago, back in
Illinois, I used to stop and pause at those places. It was as
if the soul had lifted up from the town and left it a husk,
empty and void. The breeze lifted ever so slightly the leaves
of the one poplar in front of the library building, the
benches empty. The police were behind me.

Did I say it was a strange day? Did I say the soul had
lifted from the town, flung her wings over the confluences
and diversions of the Hudson River? Did I say the dusty
bones of the dead lay over the sidewalks like cleaned ash,
the talc remains of chins and teeth and brows?

My search was going along fine as I passed the book-
store, where a mother pushed a stroller over the curb, working her elbows to get the front wheels up gently so as not
to disturb the baby inside, a small white form floating amid
blankets. Past her, at the bus stop, in front of the defunct
playhouse, shredded posters quivering, two black women

stood with that strange lonely anticipation I always see in those waiting for the bus to the George Washington Bridge: the hopelessness, their eyes gazing down the street with such longing. Past them, on the left-hand side, someone was hunched over, tying his laces with the slow deliberation of a child, as if learning the knot for the first time—certainly a fine gesture but over before I passed. He became a businessman in a long, lean, blue suit, straightening himself up, adjusting the fall of his pant cuffs, looking once to check his black polished oxfords.

To delineate the obvious, to consecrate that scene, the pure gesture, that before me appeared on the short narrow steps, three in all, leading into the front door of the funeral parlor, covered by the heavy shadows of the large pin oak growing out front: They were there out front of Olsen's establishment. A man and a woman embraced by grief. Embracing. The man in a sports coat and blue jeans with that stooped expression, slightly bent beneath some gravitational weight of his own grief; the woman in a long violet dress tightening then loosening against her hips as the breeze rippled the fabric—those hips I'll never forget, I suppose, jutting lightly against his own, as much a part of the embrace as anything. She bent and shifted with the great forces against her the way someone on the deck of a boat must adjust himself to a changing horizon—it was right there before me, the gyroscope of their pain holding the gesture, making it as pure as carved stone, petrified forever, the brass rails holding up the canopy overhead, green-and-white-striped. Suddenly a blinding purplish brilliance lit the front of the parlor afire. I was past. It was behind me. That beloved, graven gesture—near perfect—

was gone, faded off into some infinite point along the lines of my life, dissolved by time and by the human movement. I felt then, acutely, and for the first time in years, the sorrow of my loss. I headed around the block, hoping the gesture would still be there when I returned. It was the kind of frail, stupid hope that can only betray. The man and the woman by this time would have shifted into some other position. He'd be smoking a cigarette against the brass rail; she'd have her neck bent as she studied the undersides of the leaves. Ah, the mutual sadness of loss, the dead and gone. I went around the block anyway.

By the time I returned, traffic was clogged and men and women with headset radios were guiding crowds. This time I saw the klieg lights set up on the side of the street opposite Olsen's establishment, and the snaking electrical cables draped over the curbing, and the bored and lonely extras with their unreal eyes, chewing catered bagels from fold-up tables near the library. Down one dusty side street trailers were parked head to head. It was an impingement on my town's soul, a final affront. The town had given itself over to the unreal. The unreal was stopping traffic, attracting gawkers. Gawkers were more concerned with the unreal than with their own lives. The work of my later life was coming to a head. Was I to be betrayed or to be a betrayer? Were there not obligations to the dead that had to be taken into consideration, punishments to be doled out? Was it not a crime to grieve, falsely grieve, and in that false bereavement to create what is essentially a perfect human gesture? What else was I to do? What choice did I have? I aimed. The wheel jittered under my fingertips.

The curb offered up firm resistance, but my speed surmounted it. I struck the camera head-on. It lifted skyward, blocky and heavy. With a death, I made hallow the setting in which the perfect gesture took place.

And so you see my acts were not, as some have said, those of a madman. The police found no skid marks and drew their conclusions. The trial, as dictated by our fair Constitution, was quick and thorough. That third perfect gesture is there forever, where all gesture hunters keep these things, engraved on the rock of my eyelids like some ancient petroglyph. I can't get rid of it no matter how false it was. For at least a few blocks it gave me back the sorrow that was rightfully mine.

I hadn't planned in any manner to kill the director, despite the fact that death has come into my life in many ways and forms to take from me the one who provided me with the perfect gestures that, held still on the back of my eyelids, remain my salvation: my son's gesture in the stream, the heavy wash of water against our waders, and that other one in which he was in the tub, gleaming sheens of water over his smooth baby belly, the pink whiteness of his pure skin and baby fat, the lifting of his tiny hands to splash water, not knowing perhaps that it was water at all but just a warm semblance of material wrapped around his body, because at that time his eyes were still new and hard-pressed to focus on anything and had that brown-black fuzziness of the unknowing. That was all it was, a simple splashing of another element while I sat with him on the rim of the blue tub. It seized me and sent me reeling, knowing full well that what I was seeing would never repeat itself and was certainly the most beautiful sight in the world. The water boiled up around his fist. The slick oily light slid off his skin. His smiling face looked up at me, and his tiny fleck of hair lay pasted to his scalp while my wife, behind me in the hall, softly folded a towel over her arm and outside the summer air moved, tainted with lavender.

ASSORTED
FIRE EVENTS

THE FIRST house he torched that day went up in beautiful colors, fantastic, bright, lasting for an hour before the fire department got there. It didn't matter. The three feet of snow on the ground rendered their tire chains useless. Best thing was vinyl siding: burning hot as it gooped and melted, flames sweeping the sides with fantastic swiftness. A house is built from the outside in, but fire makes its way from the inside out, eagerly, until there is no more inside and just outside. That's what he liked about it. He stood for a long time watching as the conifers near the house turned brown and wilted, a ring of melted, steaming snow delineating the zone of most intense heat. The footprints he left went up into the woods, looped around back to the grounds of the summer association, large Victorian cottages along the shore of Lake Michigan, maintained by Chicago folk (as his old man said), held frozen in time by codes and bylaws; then in his old snowmobile boots he waded through the drifts to the road and made a run for it. [1]

There is nothing particularly funny about fire. Nothing to tickle the funnybone, I had to articulate it to myself in this way because I couldn't stop laughing. I'm a talker, when it's to myself, but when it's to someone else I shut up tight. The thing that would get me laughing is the sound of the fire—the amplification of it, the crackle; because it's that loud. I mean it's fantastically loud when the whole cottage is going rip-roaring up. No other sound like it on earth, lively and spunky, like popcorn in hot oil, right before the kernels explode—that tension in the sizzle, you know. The good thing is up here with the snow and the seclusion and all the summer folk down in Chicago, you can burn three or four in a row without much worry. Best is the way such a small little lick of flame can enlarge itself, branching out until it's just one big motherfucking rip-roaring beast, you know.

[1] When I was about thirteen, some guy burned several of the cottages in Bay View, a resort in northern Michigan. In the spring, when the snow melted, they were found. The one next to my grandparents' was torched, reduced to black char. I loved the sight, and found a place for it in my line-up of memorable images. In particular, I liked the way the huge pine trees all around the cottage were reduced to brittle towers.

. .

In the backyard the kids are playing, maybe seven or eight—the number not mattering because some inner-ear part of him picks up specifically his kids as he sits in the study writing, but the voices are high— the one named Gomer making rebel hoots from the sound of it; that kid Gomer who comes over sometimes (his real name is something else, like Ronald, or Rupert) to share a Popsicle with Stan, bleeding streaks of food coloring along the corners of his mouth, purposely letting it drip like that. Against the sound of Gomer's hoots, it comes; not exactly like a giant weed whacker (that's the metaphor he uses later, groping for a similar sound), more like a huge hunk of brittle cellophane crumpled by the hand of God (he'd never use that one). First the kids see the big wall of flames through the trees and between the houses, and then when the wind comes around, the smoke tart with burning plastics, polymers being reduced to carbon compounds, that gets them running, hooting and hollering with joy to the scene, first ones there, dancing and shouting because the flames are stabbing all the way up into the sky above the trees, and the smoke is drilling in the direction of the Hudson; down in town there is the guttural, archaic sound of the fire horn grunting out its pathetic call to arms. Shortly, the volunteer crew arrives, happy to be engaged with the real thing for a change. (They burned the old hospital wing, which was being torn down, for practice, two suffering from smoke inhalation.) Right off, seeing the varnish cans on the front porch and learning of the brushes that sat wet with the rags in the sun, the chief knew the cause. This was spontaneous combustion.[2]

Alone in the quiet of a late afternoon, the brushes nudge each other, soothingly lean into the pile of rags, whispering comments in a soft little sizzle and a thin swirl of smoke, which combines with the dry silence of a neighborhood where most are at work, closing deals, down in the city, doing what has to be done. The brushes talk, the can of varnish bakes, its lid rusted with speckles of rainfall oxidation. The porch was coated on Saturday. Now it's Wednesday and the snuggling brushes, drunk with the elixir of the varnish, are ready to burst forth in the song of fire.

Shank had to tie the dog down, mouth taped shut, stake it to the ground like a tent and then get the gas can and swirl it around knowing damn well that to touch the match would put himself in as much danger as the dog but going at it with systematic care anyhow with the others hanging back watching and laughing and making light of the darkness of Shank's desire to burn things alive; the point is getting them alive, like taking a lobster and plunging it in the pot (Shank's old man is a lobsterman), as if you could count the number of nerve cells, as if you could make an exact record of each fused dendrite. A blue hazy flame rolls around his ankles and the air and then bursts into the dog who, even through the tape, makes a sort of high,

[2] Last spring a house near me was reduced to rubble when it caught fire, and indeed, I was writing and heard a strange sound outside—high cellophane ruffling—and the kids were jumping for joy.

yearning squeak while the flames devour his coat and then his skin and then his body, writhing in heat-wave distortion. No one is sure which was the distortion of the heat and which was the dog's movement, so much like the monks doing their sit-down self-immolating dances during Nam.

One morning in Rochester, my aunt—mother of five, member of a fine upstanding family with no deep-felt hardships (apparent from outside), on the way to her job at the high school—took a can of gasoline, placed it in her car, drove to a quiet cul-de-sac and poured the gas over head and body and lit herself on fire. She died a few hours later, flesh consumed.[3]

The note she left was written in the first person, from the point of view of the gas can, speaking of the sloshing ride, lodged behind the driver's seat, the floor strewn with candy bar wrappers, then being gripped tightly in her long fingers and embraced against her blue dress, carried out to the end of the street where the air was cool and fresh and smelled of the juniper bush behind them; then the relief of having its soul poured from the long corrugated spout, the air hissing through her small yellow intake valve as it rushed in to replace the fluids—that great draining piss of gas out of her belly—and the clunking kettle-drum thud as she was dropped to the side carefully, with a delicateness very much appreciated. The note she wrote mulled

[3] This is horrible, tragic fact. It made the *Times*.

the trials and tribulations of life as a gas can, servicing mainly small engines of the lawn mower variety, being left out on the lawn in the hard heat of summer afternoons, on occasion being taken into the back of the boat to service the small motor, oil mixed in for that; it was a can's life, a life of being filled, emptied, tapped and shaken, refilled and checked. The gold curl of the liquid inside, upon which floated bits of grass chaff. Always the vapors pushing up against the roof of your mouth, singing, making little arias to the instability of their bonds.[4]

Those old movie newsreels of World War II flamethrowers spewing their lovely tongues into Jap-filled foxholes: long flexing membranes of combustion tearing into the bland dullness of the black and white. Lovely. Lovely.

The plot of fire is nebulous and serene, wildly fanatic and calm at the same time, trailing up curtains and along the undersides of carpet padding, taking its own sweet time and then conversely becoming diametric, logarithmic, taking big gulping gorging sweeps of the floorboards and runners—until it sings sweetly the fantastic house-burning lament, blasting out of windows and licking the roof eaves. You drive up to it stunned and bent over with anguish at the very central fact that what was once around your life—objects of so-called sentimental attachment—is now ash.

. .

---

[4] This is fiction.

Burning things came naturally to Fenton, and he did so whenever and wherever he could. His father assured his mother that it was the natural proclivity of a boy to touch a flame to things. As a kid I did so myself, he assured her. It was a phase the boy would outgrow, he added. The rocket ship was makeshift, a couple of tubes of cardboard taped together and stuffed with wax paper (Fenton was sure that nothing burned better than wax paper), capped by a crude twisted cone of construction paper—dark blue, all jury-rigged to a small slab of plywood. It was the gas. He doused the tubing with gas and then the board and laid it near the side of the garage—in that narrow space between his garage and the neighbor's—then doused a bit more for good measure, counting, five, four, three, two, one, touching the Bic lighter to the edge of the wood, not feeling the lick, the vibration, the uplift of flame—the small barely visible violet underside of the fume-flame touching his tube socks and gathering around the cuff of his jeans, with a combustion point higher than the hair on his ankles— flame opening to flame itself taking one big heaving pop, gulp, and then roaring up to his face, flinching back, falling forward into it, catching his jeans and his socks and up his leg before he knew what was what, and the dry wood along the garage, too; it had been a long dry summer in which the whole region was baked crisp. It was near fall anyhow, that tart dry smell holding the portents of what was going to happen on the first cold frost-snap night. It was all in a half second, until he was on fire doing the STOP, DROP, ROLL thing just as he'd been trained. (In class they had gone over it, throw the blanket over the body or if you're alone don't panic and run but roll on the ground.) But there wasn't room between the two garages, and he rolled back against the neighbor's wall and then towards the fire—screaming all the while this high, dog-whistle-pitched squeal that couldn't be heard anyhow because, across the alley that serviced the driveways of this small Midwestern town, Mr. Jones was roaring swaths of grass with his ill-tuned Lawn Boy, drowning out the screams and the first crackles of the fire. He'd be the first to notice the smoke, first to see it, but too late because by that time both garages were engulfed. (He was hard of hearing but his eyesight was a resolute twenty-twenty.) The inferno would soon leap the garage to the porch and, before the fire trucks could arrive, take the whole side of Fenton's house and part of the neighbor's, too, destroying both with enough smoke damage to call them total losses on the insurance rosters.

Fenton's skin is actually giving off smoke, a swamp misting in the early morn, crawling on all fours, looking slightly ridiculous if you were to view it impartially, as if in a movie, knowing it was an actor in a fire suit, some stunt person like a Chaplin tramp, or in blackface, fireface—really, honestly, smoking skin burning still, not able to scream now for the effort he has to put into moving away from the fire that is moving rapidly (following the soft westerly breeze)—but he can sense it licking his heels, although he can't feel his heels because the soles of his sneakers have melted into his feet, or what remains of them; it's a ghastly sight that no one gets to see. (He's a latchkey kid. Usually he goes in and switches on the TV and kills a good hour before getting his books out of his backpack.) No one is

there to see his heroic crawl out of the fire into the fresh
air, his singed lungs gasping. When the emergency rescue
guys and the fire trucks scream up to the curb he's in the
very center of the front lawn, still smoldering, like a heap
of campfire residue. But the men have seen stranger sights,
still-living souls with flames dancing out of their necks;
people dancing fire dances with their hair going like a torch,
things that defy even those whose imaginations are trained
by computer animation techniques to accept anything on
this strange earth; these guys in the course of fighting
fires—the older ones—going into roaring farmhouses full
of brittle ancient wood—have seen the fire gods make
strange faces, with licking tongues. So Fenton wasn't a
strange sight to them the way he'd be to you if you were to
come upon his smoking form. The percentage of his skin
damaged (like that of my aunt) was given as a statistic, as
if the square inches of body tissue could be charted, cubed
off, like square acres of farmland in Iowa. Anyone familiar
with the rudiments of such news stories—fire-damaged
souls who have their skin grafted in a tortuous series of
operations that are (according to many accounts) more
painful than the actual original burning; bodies hovering
in special flotation tanks, suspended in liquid, sponged
off, the wounds oozing for months and years. For anyone
familiar with such tales, the story of Fenton's struggles to
survive would be pretty routine. Like Christ, he lay in the
tank with his arms out. Like Christ, he suffered for all
humankind. Like Christ, he sucked into his skin and nerves
the pain of the entire universe. It was a holy event. Eyes
dark blue open to the ceiling tiles. His lips parted, trying
to speak. Like Christ, he walked into the hot fire of hell

and departed with only long purple blemishes and a face that was hard to recognize as human. People walked past that face with their eyes at the sky or their feet, knowing that to look at it would be to laugh out loud. It would be a big, blasting laugh that Fenton's face would produce in most people, the kind you make at the circus when the clown's dripping eyes and his goofy smile are painted over the saddest-looking, most pathetic clown-school dropout you've ever seen, some guy whose family has been in the circus for generations and has no way out except to keep doing what the family does; he hates the job more than life itself but keeps going and going, from Madison Square Garden shows to small county fairs. In the circus there is fire, too. It's spun in hoops and thrown from the mouth of God.

THE
WOODCUTTER

THE FIRST day back he began chopping like a maniac, going at the wood day and night—or so they say. He'd been back six years when I was old enough to notice him, and by that time he went a bit slower (at least that's what I was told) but still split a good cord, a full cord, in about two hours depending on what kind of wood it was and how large around the tree was; he had a gas powered wedge that halved the logs; then he just threw them into place and took a clean hard swap, usually just one chop was all it took, and then he'd swish them out of the way with his steel-toed boots and do another; all day, most days, seven days a week, barring only the worst kind of weather. When he stopped, there were usually dew drops of sweat and condensation on his black beard; in cold weather, a dangling clot of ice; in the summer there was a fine little braid of red welts under the hairs and just above the skin. Prickly heat. The lumberjack shirt he wore, traditional red and black Pendleton of good wool, graced him deep into summer. When he killed himself—August 1, 1985—he was in the shirt, next to a fresh cord of seasoned oak stacked against his garage. His wife was out there undoing the buttons slowly to get to the wound, small and round, produced by a teflon-coated bullet (the papers said) that eased neatly into his chest and right out, lickety split, the wonders of moon-shot technology going a step further than nonstick pans (my father muttered). Theories abounded about the exact reason, but suicide being an unexplainable enigma it didn't take much to put most of it on Nam, on his role in the siege at Khe Sanh, on buddies lost and all that, although the papers mentioned he was being sued for taking down a red maple on private property without permission, going right up the Jansons' driveway (one of those washed gravel loops to the front of their cedar-sided ranch), tying a rope around the tree and then his pickup hook, getting the chain saw revved up, and then telling me to ease up on the clutch when he gave a shout (being only fourteen I wasn't versed in the workings of a manual shift, but I did as I was told, easing up slowly, and the truck jerked back, and the tree went down behind me with a loud, dust-clouded whomp). Before I was out of the truck's cab, he was slicing into the large trunk, getting right into the heart of the tree, which was a good hundred and twenty years old according to my ring count (later). I kept quiet about my role in his demise. It wouldn't do to let people know that maybe it wasn't Nam that caused him to shoot a nice, neat hole in his heart, and that maybe it was just other stuff, the value of trees being dissembled, the wonderful easing up of weight when the head of the ax left the arch and pulled him into the chop. (I'd watched a million times.) The threat of not being able to go into the forested yards of his neighbors, or the local parks where he got most of the trees, to take down the excess growth, was too much for him; his lumberjack days were numbered.

Printed by RR Donnelley at Glasgow, UK